A stalker on the loose . . .

Finally the service was over. I felt exhausted and achy. Ever since Gina died, I'd had trouble sleeping. When I dozed off my sleep was fitful, filled with nightmares. Once I'd dreamed that someone was sneaking up behind me with a big syringe. I woke up just as I turned and saw the needle about to plunge into my shoulder.

On the way back to the mental health center I picked up a vegetable sub and Diet Coke to eat at my desk. I would have loved to go home for a badly needed nap, but there was too much work waiting in my office . . .

I'd already started returning phone calls before I saw the other message. It was on the far left corner of my desk, a folded paper on the opposite side from the other notes.

I stopped dialing, set down the receiver. With shaking hands I opened the note. Stared at the page of typing paper with the bold black-marker message. DON'T THINK I'VE FORGOTTEN YOU. YOU'LL PAY FOR WHAT YOU DID.

Don't miss

CRY FOR HELP

the thrilling debut by
Karen Hanson Stuyck!

MORE MYSTERIES FROM THE BERKLEY PUBLISHING GROUP . . .

THE HERON CARVIC MISS SEETON MYSTERIES: Retired art teacher Miss Seeton steps in where Scotland Yard stumbles. "A most beguiling protagonist!"
—*New York Times*

by Heron Carvic
MISS SEETON SINGS
MISS SEETON DRAWS THE LINE
WITCH MISS SEETON
PICTURE MISS SEETON
ODDS ON MISS SEETON

by Hampton Charles
ADVANTAGE MISS SEETON
MISS SEETON AT THE HELM
MISS SEETON, BY APPOINTMENT

by Hamilton Crane
HANDS UP, MISS SEETON
MISS SEETON CRACKS THE CASE
MISS SEETON PAINTS THE TOWN
MISS SEETON BY MOONLIGHT
MISS SEETON ROCKS THE CRADLE
MISS SEETON GOES TO BAT
MISS SEETON PLANTS SUSPICION
STARRING MISS SEETON
MISS SEETON UNDERCOVER
MISS SEETON RULES
SOLD TO MISS SEETON

KATE SHUGAK MYSTERIES: A former D.A. solves crimes in the far Alaska north . . .

by Dana Stabenow
A COLD DAY FOR MURDER
DEAD IN THE WATER
A FATAL THAW
A COLD-BLOODED BUSINESS
PLAY WITH FIRE

INSPECTOR BANKS MYSTERIES: Award-winning British detective fiction at its finest . . . "Robinson's novels are habit-forming!"—*West Coast Review of Books*

by Peter Robinson
THE HANGING VALLEY
WEDNESDAY'S CHILD
INNOCENT GRAVES
PAST REASON HATED
FINAL ACCOUNT

CASS JAMESON MYSTERIES: Lawyer Cass Jameson seeks justice in the criminal courts of New York City in this highly acclaimed series . . . "A witty, gritty heroine."
—*New York Post*

by Carolyn Wheat
FRESH KILLS
MEAN STREAK
DEAD MAN'S THOUGHTS

SCOTLAND YARD MYSTERIES: Featuring Detective Superintendent Duncan Kincaid and his partner, Sergeant Gemma James . . . "Charming!"
—*New York Times Book Review*

by Deborah Crombie
A SHARE IN DEATH
LEAVE THE GRAVE GREEN
ALL SHALL BE WELL

LIZ JAMES MYSTERIES: Featuring Liz James, public relations officer for the Houston Mental Health Center. Now she has her work cut out for her as someone targets clinic employees for murder . . .

by Karen Hanson Stuyck
CRY FOR HELP
HELD ACCOUNTABLE

HELD ACCOUNTABLE

Karen Hanson Stuyck

BERKLEY PRIME CRIME, NEW YORK

HELD ACCOUNTABLE

A Berkley Prime Crime Book / published by arrangement with the author

PRINTING HISTORY
Berkley Prime Crime edition / September 1996

For information address: The Berkley Publishing Group, 200 Madison Avenue, New York, New York 10016.

The Putnam Berkley World Wide Web site address is
http://www.berkley.com

ISBN: 0-425-15466-1

Berkley Prime Crime Books are published
by The Berkley Publishing Group,
200 Madison Avenue, New York, NY 10016.

PRINTED IN THE UNITED STATES OF AMERICA

10 9 8 7 6 5 4 3 2 1

In loving memory of my parents,
Sig and Mildred Hess Hanson

HELD ACCOUNTABLE

Chapter One

I WALKED DOWN THE HALL OF THE HOUSTON MENTAL Health Center, carrying my newly filled, fire-engine red coffee mug. It had been a long, trying day, and my taste buds were already anticipating the first hit of sweet, creamy coffee.

"Excuse me, miss," a deep voice behind me said.

I turned. The man was too well dressed to be a psychiatrist and too affluent-looking to be one of the center's patients. "Can I help you?" I asked the tall, very tan, thirtysomething man in the $1,000 suit.

He grinned, flashing large white teeth at me. "As a matter of fact, you can. I'm looking for Gina Lawrence. Can you tell me where her office is?"

I don't know why I hesitated. There was nothing overtly threatening about the man, and my usual instinct was to lead an inquirer to the desired office. I was, after all, the center's public relations officer, and this man was certainly a representative of the public. "Gina works upstairs in the adult clinic," I finally said. "The receptionist will page her for you."

The man's smile did not falter. "Thanks. Right up there?" He pointed to the stairs. "You don't happen to know her office number, do you? I want to surprise her. I'm an old college friend, Stan Baker." He offered me his hand.

I shook it. ''Hi, I'm Liz James. But no, right offhand I don't know Gina's office number.'' I did know that her office was directly above mine, both of us in the building's southwest corner. I'd been there dozens of times. This was not, however, information I intended to share with Stan.

''I looked for her car in the parking lot in back,'' Stan continued, ''but I didn't see it.''

This guy was starting to remind me of an overly aggressive salesman, someone who worked at an upscale place like a BMW dealership. ''Maybe she's out to lunch,'' I lied, unwilling to tell him that Gina parked in the garage across the street. ''Nice meeting you.'' I turned toward my office.

''Yeah, thanks for your help,'' Stan said as he moved toward the stairs.

The minute I was in my office I phoned Gina. No answer. Then I remembered. One of Gina's battered wives' groups met Tuesday afternoons. Probably she was in the group now. A good sign: Stan wouldn't be any more successful in finding her than I was. And who knows? Maybe he really was an old friend of hers. In any case, he could leave a message.

After that I kicked off my shoes, drank my coffee, and tried to relax. It didn't work. I kept remembering what Gina had said to me this morning at the employee recognition program. ''It's kind of nice to be around some women who aren't all scared shitless that her old man is about to make good on his promise to kill her.''

Half an hour later Gina still wasn't answering her phone. I decided I needed more caffeine; never mind that I had promised myself I was going to cut down any day now.

The coffeepot was in one of the human resources offices at the opposite end of my hall. Lauren Jones, a pretty brunette file clerk only recently out of high school, looked up when I walked in. "Hi, Liz. Congratulations on that award you got today," she said.

"Thanks." I poured my coffee and dumped in fake cream and artificial sweetener, asking my body to forgive me. "I don't know if you'd call it an award though. I just didn't move on to a better-paying job."

"I can't believe you've worked here for ten years," Lauren said.

I grinned. Ten years ago Lauren had probably been in third grade. "I can't either," I admitted. In fact, the thought of being in one job for that long—ten of the eleven years since I'd graduated from college—was oddly depressing.

"Well, I'm sure not going to stick around that long," Lauren said just as her boss, Donna Hubbard, marched into the office.

Donna pretended not to have heard her. A tall woman with a lacquered helmet of Texas "big hair," she was the kind of person who always wore dress-for-success suits to work. "Oh, hello, Liz," she said, "I didn't know you were here." Her chilly look said what her words didn't: Another five minutes of potential working time wasted and, by God, no one but Donna Hubbard even cared!

I left. After picking up my mail and stopping in the rest room, I was back in my office. It took me a few minutes to see the folded piece of typing paper on the edge of my desk. Curious, I picked it up.

Inside, printed in big block letters, were the words: IT'S YOUR FAULT, BITCH. I HOLD YOU ACCOUNTABLE.

WHAT WAS my fault? What had I done? I tried to recall any major arguments with coworkers. Whose feelings had

I hurt? Was there someone I'd unintentionally harmed? What was I being held accountable for? The only person who I knew for sure hated my guts was in no position to deliver messages to my office. Could this be some kind of sick prank?

It was a big relief when half an hour later I spotted Gina in the hall. I waved her into my office, only too happy to focus on someone else's problems for a few minutes.

"What's up?" she asked, standing in the doorway.

I told her about encountering her old friend Stan Baker.

"Who?" She looked confused.

I repeated the name. "He said he was a friend from college. Wanted to know where your office was. I told him to have Missy page you."

Suddenly Gina's sharply planed face turned alert. Suspicious. "What did this guy look like?"

"Tall, blond, well-dressed." I tried to remember anything else. "Looked like he works out. Maybe twenty-nine, thirty."

"He kind of remind you of a salesman? Charming in a hearty, bullshitty sort of way?"

I nodded. "You *do* know him then?"

"Yeah." Gina's husky voice was suddenly grim, her face a shade paler than usual. "My ex-husband, whose name, incidentally, is Todd Murdock, not Stan Baker." Gina searched the hallway, as if expecting the man to leap out at us from one of the offices. "Shit! I didn't know he was in Houston. He's probably the asshole who kept phoning last night and hanging up whenever I answered. I finally unplugged the phone at 2 a.m."

"Should we notify security?" I asked. "Security" in this case was one of several moonlighting HPD police officers.

"And say what?" Gina's tone was bitter. "Listen, Liz, I never got any restraining order to keep him away from me. I just did what I tell my clients to do: I got the hell out and made sure I went someplace where the bastard couldn't find me."

I finished the thought for her. "Except now he has."

Gina nodded. "It sure looks that way." She turned and started up the stairs, looking like a death row inmate whose last-ditch request for a pardon has just been turned down.

She phoned me half an hour later. "Nobody up here has seen Todd. Missy said she's sure he didn't ask for me at the clinic this afternoon; she was at the reception desk all day." Gina sounded more in control now. Her voice had lost the edge of panic I'd heard earlier.

"So what are you going to do?" I asked.

"I'm going to go about business as usual." She made it sound as if I'd just asked her if she planned to stop breathing. "And I think I'm going to try to sleep somewhere else tonight."

"You can stay at my place," I offered. "I've got an extra bedroom with a fairly comfortable couch." The couch was all that was left of the furniture from my former marriage. Max and I had bought the sofa, a clunky-looking oatmeal tweed number that converted into a queen-sized bed, so that his mother had a place to sleep when she came to visit. I would be glad for someone I liked to have a chance to sleep on it.

Gina hesitated. Then, "Thanks. You're sure it won't inconvenience you?"

"I'm sure." We agreed to meet at 5:15 to pick up her clothes, then drive to my apartment.

I phoned Nick at the *Chronicle* to tell him I had to cancel our dinner plans. Nick Finley and I had been dating, on and off, for about a year now, but in the last month, without either of us discussing it, we'd started getting together almost every night.

"Let me come with you when you go to Gina's apartment," he said when I told him about Todd. "The guy might be waiting for her there."

I smiled. As I'd punched in Nick's office number, I'd envisioned how my ex-husband Max would have reacted to the news that Gina was spending the night. "You know how exhausted I am when I get home from work, Liz, and the last thing I want to see when I walk in the door is some stranger camping out in our living room. And what if this deranged husband shows up at our place? Did you ever think of that?"

But Nick, bless his heart, had only wanted to help. I felt as if I'd heard a message from above: See? He's totally unlike that self-absorbed jerk you were married to.

Still, much as I appreciated Nick's offer of assistance, I didn't think that Gina would like the idea of traveling with an entourage of bodyguards. "It's nice of you to offer," I said, "but I think we'll be okay by ourselves. We'll only be there for a few minutes, and I don't think Todd will pull anything if he sees she has someone with her."

Nick did not sound convinced, but he didn't belabor his point (another *major* difference from Max). "If you change your mind, page me. Otherwise I'll talk to you tonight, maybe come over, if that's okay."

"I'd like that." I smiled as I hung up.

I spent the remainder of the afternoon finishing the copy for the new issue of the mental health center's newsletter. I wasn't exactly in a writing mood, but the fact that I had to send my disk off to the layout artist tomorrow spurred me into action. I've always told myself that I write best (or at least fastest) when threatened by an approaching deadline. This, of course, is also a rationalization for a major procrastination problem, but the system works for me.

The knock on my open door startled me. I looked up to see Gina, then glanced at my watch. "Is it that time already?"

I studied her face. She didn't look scared, but there was a tightness around her mouth and a flatness in her hazel eyes.

We decided to take both cars to her apartment. Gina's body tensed as we stepped out the back door of the center into the parking lot. Todd/Stan was nowhere in sight. We walked to my car, and I drove the two of us to the parking garage across the street.

"Todd didn't try to contact you again?" I asked. I hadn't realized how nervous I'd been feeling on the trek through the parking lot until the two of us were safely locked inside my car. My body suddenly went limp.

"No. I had three groups today, so I was out of my office a lot. But if Todd called, he didn't leave a message, and Missy said the only people who asked for me were clients."

We were at her car now, a tan Nova. Gina scanned the garage before she got out. Hurriedly she slid into the driver's seat, and relocked her door. Before she turned on the ignition, she even checked the backseat.

I followed her out of the garage, down the street until we were out of the Texas Medical Center, with its back-to-back hospitals and medical training facilities, heading toward Montrose.

At the outskirts of the medical complex, we passed Hermann Park, where a few kids were still playing on the swings, taking advantage of the mild March weather. I knew that on the other side of the huge park mothers would be coaxing cranky toddlers into leaving the zoo. "Come on, sweetie, it's dinnertime now. We've got to go home." The zoo, the duck pond, and the open-air train that circled the park—all of these were real to me. I'd been there dozens of times with my nieces and nephew and my godson, Jonathan Marshall. It was the threat of danger that seemed unreal on this lush spring day, like the sound of a gunshot during a concert in the park. I wanted to believe that it wasn't true, that Todd meant Gina no harm, that all was right with the world. But the look on Gina's face as she got out of my car was still too vivid to let me buy it.

Gina lived in Montrose, an area close to downtown that managed to encompass a variety of older brick homes, a large gay population, and lots of antique shops, New Age stores, and a wide selection of restaurants. Gina's apartment was on a block filled with two-story brick houses that had mainly been converted into duplexes. At the end of the block (thanks to Houston's no-zoning policy) was a convenience store.

Gina parked on the street. I pulled up behind her and got out, feeling tense.

We walked together, silently, Gina gripping her key like a weapon until we reached the azalea bushes near the front door. The only person I spotted while Gina unlocked her door was a woman with long, mousy-brown hair carrying two bags of groceries.

"I'll only be a minute," Gina said when we were inside. I followed her up the stairs.

I'd been to her place several times, yet every time I saw

it I was struck with how sparsely furnished her apartment was. In the living room there were half a dozen metal folding chairs and some oversized floor pillows to accommodate the support group meetings Gina sometimes held in her home. The dining room contained a table, two wooden chairs, and a battered desk and chair that looked as if they'd come from the Salvation Army.

Gina's only concession to the concept of interior decorating were her plants. Her windowsills held pots of ivy, lush ferns, even a couple of African violets. Hanging baskets of flowering hibiscus hung in front of her living room window, and two huge dieffenbachias shared the floor with the pillows and folding chairs.

"Is there anything I can do?" I asked while I watched her throw clothes and toiletries into an old Samsonite suitcase.

"Yeah, water the plants on the sill in the dining room. There's some water on the kitchen counter that I left out to oxygenate."

I found the old plastic milk carton filled with water and started watering. It crossed my mind that Gina's clothes were as spartan and functional as her home furnishings: simple, solid-colored separates—black and gray slacks, a couple of white blouses, inexpensive red and navy blazers—that she could interchange with everything else she owned. She wore a watch and big gold hoop pierced earrings, but no other jewelry. I'd never seen her wear make-up, and her shoulder-length auburn hair was badly in need of a trim. She was a woman who clearly couldn't care less how she looked, but she was so beautiful—a delicate, high-cheekboned face with pale, flawless skin; a strong, slender body—that she looked good no matter what she wore.

Gina appeared with her suitcase and an armload of manila folders. She headed for the living room window and scanned the street. "Okay, I'm ready," she said.

I offered to carry the suitcase, and the two of us started down the stairs. My heart thudded against my chest as Gina unlocked the door.

I didn't see anyone when I stepped outside. Dusk had descended while we were in her apartment. I took a couple of deep breaths and told myself my impulse to run to my car was irrational.

Until I spotted him, Todd/Stan Baker, stalking to the door. Wearing designer jeans and a yellow polo shirt now. He nodded curtly at me. I couldn't tell if he recognized me from the mental health center. "Gina," he said, moving toward her, smiling, "how you doing, hon?"

He kind of drawled the words, not Southern-sounding exactly. More terminally laid-back. Todd sounded like a man who'd been told his entire life how charming he was. The Grade A bullshitter.

Gina flinched but said in an even voice, "I'm fine, Todd. And now I'm leaving. I don't have anything more I want to say to you."

"But what if *I* have something I want to say to *you*?" He moved closer. Stopped smiling. Lost the drawl too.

"Call my lawyer," Gina said. "She'll relay the message." She started toward her car.

Todd lunged and grabbed her arm. "Hey, I'm talking to you."

I stood behind them, frozen. I noticed that Todd wore a diamond-studded Rolex on his right wrist.

"Get your fucking hands off me!" Gina screamed.

Her words unlocked my brain. "I'm calling the police," I announced loudly, heading for the cellular phone in my car.

Todd strode past me, his blandly handsome face transformed by fury. "I'll be back, bitch," he shouted over his shoulder. "Don't think you've heard the last of me."

Gina was standing where he'd left her, her face expressionless. I ran to her. "You okay?"

I wasn't sure she heard me. I touched her arm. "Gina?"

At last her eyes seemed to focus on me. I repeated my question.

She nodded. But she didn't look okay. She looked like somebody who'd been sick for a long time and hadn't completely recovered yet.

I ran to the curb, just in time to see Todd drive away in a navy Seville, moving too fast for me to get the license number.

I offered to drive Gina back to my place; we could come get her car tomorrow. But she insisted she wanted to drive herself.

I got into my car and locked all the doors. As I pulled into traffic I noticed my hand was shaking when I shifted gears. I kept checking my rearview mirror to make sure that Gina was still behind me. At every intersection I expected a navy Seville to dart out at us.

Chapter Two

I DEAD-BOLTED THE FRONT DOOR THE MINUTE WE WERE inside my apartment, feeling as if I'd just finished a marathon. I showed Gina the extra bedroom, then hurried back to the living room window to see if Todd had followed us. There was no sign of him. Yet.

I was pouring myself a glass of Chablis when Gina walked into the kitchen. "I decided I need a drink. How about you?"

She shook her head. "No, thanks, though I'd like a glass of water."

I poured her a glass from the plastic container I keep in the refrigerator, then inspected the Swiss cheese, hunk of salami, and box of crackers I'd placed on the kitchen counter. "Oh, hell, you only eat vegetables and grains, right?" Every time we'd gone to lunch Gina had eaten a green salad and whole wheat roll.

She smiled. "No, I'm only prissy about alcohol and drugs. Red meat, cholesterol, and white sugar I can live with." As if to prove her point, she started cutting the salami and then nibbled on a piece while she sliced the cheese.

We took our drinks and the plate of crackers and cheese to the living room. After the starkness of Gina's apartment, my own place felt warmly familiar: full of comfortable, upholstered furniture; bright prints; and framed photographs of my family, my sister's three kids, and my godchild. Maybe the wine was having its effect too, or perhaps I was just feeling less fearful. Todd didn't seem like the type who'd try to break in the door, I reassured myself. He'd want to talk his way in. And since I had absolutely no intention of opening the door tonight to anyone I hadn't known for years, I began to feel, well, almost safe.

Gina was eating the cheese and salami and crackers like a woman who'd missed lunch. "This is good," she said, after washing down a mouthful of crackers with water. "When I'm nervous," she explained, "I eat."

"Funny," I said, "when I'm nervous is one of the few times I don't want to eat. Instead I eat when I'm sad or angry or depressed or happy or bored."

Gina smiled. "Yeah, I like to eat when I'm happy too. To celebrate." She piled both kinds of cheese and a slice of salami on top of a cracker. "Here's to getting away from Todd." She popped the cracker sandwich into her mouth.

I helped myself to a slice of salami. After losing thirty-five pounds last year, my relationship with food was still tenuous. "So you think Todd's going to give up on you and go back home to California?"

"Eventually." When she stopped chewing, her face was grim. "But knowing Todd, he won't leave until he puts me through hell first."

"What do you think he wants from you anyway?"

"He *says* he wants me to come back to him." When I looked surprised, Gina added, "He doesn't really want me back. We argued twenty-four hours a day. That's why he started beating me, said I was a smart-ass." She shook her head, making her thick hair tumble over her face. "It's the principle of the thing with Todd. Me leaving him was like having his BMW decide it wanted a new owner. Todd figured I was his possession until *he* decided it was time to trade me in for a new model.''

''But why is he doing this now? You've been divorced for—what, five years? I mean, I can remember feeling pretty crazed right after my divorce too, but five years later most people have moved on.''

Gina shrugged. ''Todd isn't most people. I wish I'd realized that before I married the schmuck, but you know the way you are when you're young and infatuated—you just see what you want to see. I look back now at some of the things Todd pulled when we were dating. One time he punched this guy for pulling into a parking space that Todd wanted. Everything that went wrong was *always* somebody else's fault. He got a bad grade because the professor had it in for him, not because he'd stayed out partying the night before and never got around to studying. His car was totaled because the idiot in the other car hadn't yielded when Todd ran the red light.''

She shook her head, looking disgusted. ''I mean, what did I need? A neon sign saying 'Don't marry this man! He is terminally adolescent'?'' Gina leaned forward and made another cracker sandwich.

I picked up the empty plate. ''Want me to cut some more cheese? Or maybe I should start dinner.'' I searched my mind for what I had in the refrigerator that could be made into a quick meal.

Gina held up a palm. ''No, I'm stuffed. Don't make anything else on my account.''

I decided I wasn't very hungry either. Maybe later I'd make some tuna salad or an omelette. I went to the kitchen, freshened my glass of wine, and filled the plate with more cheese and crackers in case Gina was just being polite. I came back, sat down. Silence descended on us like a pocket of Houston's summer humidity.

"So," Gina said, "what's new with you, Liz?" She laughed.

I grinned. I had first met Gina when interviewing her for our newsletter—a few perfunctory paragraphs, I thought, about the new staff member. At first I'd found her serious and too intense: a woman who quoted statistics about the number of women being beaten every day in the U.S. I was used to brand-new therapists, just out of their graduate programs, being wary and pedantic in their interviews with me—a real pain in the ass. It was as if they thought they were taking an oral exam that would be circulated among their peers. Accordingly they weighted down every sentence with professional jargon. And God forbid that they reveal one iota of personal (or at least interesting) information. Gina was just the same.

"Is there any special reason you decided to work in this field?" I had finally asked her, not expecting much.

She skewered me with those piercing hazel eyes and smiled for the first time. "Hell, yes. One night my husband beat the shit out of me. Over nothing. The next morning I saw myself in the mirror—my eye swollen shut, a big bruise on my cheek. I decided right then to get out. No one deserved to live like that." She smiled, mocking herself. "Later I decided to get my master's so I could share this insight with other abused women." This was a woman, I'd thought, who I wanted to be my friend.

I told Gina now about the anonymous note I had received this afternoon.

She blinked. "You're kidding. You too?"

"You got one too?"

"About a week ago, though mine came in the mail. Envelope just said Gina Lawrence, Houston Mental Health Center. Postmarked in Houston. The note was like yours: 'I blame you, bitch, for what happened,' I think." Absently Gina pulled on a strand of her hair. "Yours was left in your office?"

I nodded.

She thought about it for a minute. "You know, my office is directly above yours. Isn't your number 101? And I'm 201. I bet somebody dropped off a letter that was meant for me in your office. It didn't have your name on it, did it?"

"No." But Gina's had. "Was your note typed or handwritten?"

"Everything was printed by hand. In big capital letters."

I let out my breath; I hadn't realized I'd been holding it.

"Written with a black marker?"

"Right. I bet it was Todd. You said he was looking for my office."

"And he was standing right outside *my* office," I said, feeling a strange rush of relief. "Only Todd saw me walk into my office; he would have known it wasn't yours."

"Maybe he put the letter there before he knew it was yours. Someone could have told him, 'Yeah, Gina's office is at the end of the hall, first one on the right.' "

I tried to think. Could the letter have been there the first time I walked in, right after talking to Todd? It was possible. I could have come in, made my phone call to Gina, drunk my coffee, and overlooked the folded paper sitting on the corner of my desk. It was only when I came back to dump my stack of mail on that particular spot that I'd noticed the letter.

''Or else Todd was pissed at me for not telling him where your office is. Maybe he left the letter when he saw me leave to get more coffee.''

Gina shook her head. ''I doubt that he had a clue you were trying to protect me.''

She was probably right. I felt a stab of something close to glee (See? Nobody hates you; nobody blames you for what you did to them) and immediately felt ashamed for feeling happy the letter was meant for Gina.

''At first I thought the message was from somebody in one of my groups or from one of the men who they ran out on,'' Gina said.

''Why would somebody from one of your groups send you a note like that? I can understand a man blaming you for his wife's leaving him, but not one of the women you're helping.''

Gina shrugged. ''Part of my job is to prod them, to cut through all the rationalizations and the yes-but-maybe-someday bullshit. Sometimes I have to give them a big shove before they start taking responsibility for changing their lives. That pisses people off. And if they leave the guy and their life seems worse—living at a crowded, noisy shelter, having money problems—some of them might blame me for that too.''

''Gee, it sounds like a great job.''

She smiled. ''Actually it is. I can sit in one of the groups and think a third, maybe half, of these women would be dead five years from now if they hadn't left the man who was abusing them. The way I see it, anything I can do to help them make the transition to an independent existence is helping save lives.''

Gina pushed a strand of auburn hair out of her face and anchored it behind her ear. ''Being angry with me is just a stage in therapy. They get over it.'' She extended her long, graceful fingers and counted on them. ''In the last five years I've worked as a therapist in a drug treatment program, an attendant on the adolescent unit at the state hospital, and a group therapist for battered women. And a large number of my clients would have loved to punch me out at one time or another. I can live with it.''

There was a knock on my front door. The two of us froze, staring at the door. Of course I knew it was Nick, I told myself as I saw him through the peephole. But if I'd been so sure, how come I now felt limp with relief?

Nick kissed me hello. ''Sorry I didn't call first. I just got out of an interview near here, and I wanted to see if everything went okay.''

''I'm glad you came.'' I started to introduce Nick to Gina, but he'd already walked up to her.

''I don't think we've met yet,'' he said, smiling at her. ''I'm Nick Finley.''

''Gina Lawrence.'' She shook the hand Nick extended but didn't smile.

''Did you have any trouble when you picked up the stuff at your apartment?'' he asked, sitting on the tan upholstered chair opposite me.

''Todd showed up just as we were leaving, but we handled it. He left and didn't follow us.''

I wondered if I was imagining her antipathy toward Nick. She wasn't overtly hostile, but her voice was flat and she kept glancing away from him when she talked. Maybe she was just reserved with strangers—or at least male strangers.

It didn't seem to bother Nick. But his next question was directed at me. "Did he threaten either of you?"

"He threatened Gina and grabbed her arm. When she started yelling at him and I said I was calling the police, he told her he'd be back another time."

"He's all talk," Gina said. "He'll probably make a lot of middle-of-the-night phone calls and send me some threatening letters. Then he'll go back to California, telling himself he really kicked ass."

I looked at her in surprise. Why was she making Todd sound so innocuous when half an hour ago she'd been expecting him to put her through hell?

"Maybe you should stay with Liz for a while until you're sure he's left town," Nick said. "Just in case he's more dangerous than you think."

Gina finally looked at him. "I'm not worried," she said. This time there was no mistaking the hostility.

It was a long evening. Nick made a couple more attempts to draw out Gina, asking her about her work at the center, how she'd ended up in Houston. Gina replied tersely, as if someone were charging her by the word for her answers. She didn't ask Nick any questions and directed the few comments she made at me.

Finally, around nine-thirty, Nick left, saying he'd call me tomorrow. A few minutes later Gina announced that she was going to bed. "I've had a lot of late evenings this week and I'm really exhausted."

She didn't have to offer me any excuses. I followed her to the study with sheets, blankets, and a pillow and showed her how to pull out the couch. "Good night, Gina."

"Night." She looked up from the sheet she was tucking in. "Thanks, Liz. Thanks for everything."

She was gone the next morning by the time I woke up at 6:45. A note on the kitchen counter said she'd gone to work early to catch up on paperwork. In the study Gina had converted her bed back into a couch, and the sheets, blankets, and pillow lay in a neat pile on the floor. She'd apparently taken her suitcase with her.

It wasn't until late in the afternoon that I saw her again. I was still rushing to write headlines for the newsletter and Gina seemed in a hurry too.

"I just wanted to thank you again for letting me spend the night," she said, standing in the doorway of my office.

"You're welcome to stay tonight too. If you're gone for a few days maybe Todd will give up."

She smiled. "I appreciate the offer, but I think I'm going to sleep on the couch in my office tonight. Todd phoned to say he was flying back to California today. I called the airline to make *sure* he really was booked on a flight this afternoon. But I guess I won't be totally convinced that he's gone until I phone his office in LA and actually hear his voice."

"Sure you don't want to spend the night at my place? It's probably more comfortable than your office."

Gina shook her head. "No, really, my couch is fine. I've slept there before." She smiled. "And this way I'll have to get caught up on my paperwork."

She glanced at her watch. "Got to go. I'm already late for my meeting." Apparently she saw the worry on my face because she leaned forward then, patting my arm. "Don't worry, Liz. I'm perfectly safe. And thanks again for last night."

"Sure. Anytime." I just hoped that Todd really had gone back to California. The man I'd seen yesterday didn't look as if he'd give up that easily.

NICK AND I went out to dinner that night at Ninfa's, our favorite Tex-Mex restaurant. I could feel myself relax as we sipped frozen margaritas and munched on tostados dunked in Ninfa's green sauce. After the waiter brought us platters of sizzling chicken fajitas, Nick told me about the story he was working on, an investigation of a medical clinic on the north side of town that was filing Medicare claims for fictitious patients. "I'm sorry, sir, I don't know nothing," the receptionist at the front desk had told him. Nick lowered his voice, imitating the woman's country twang. " 'And my boss he said to tell you he's away on vacation and won't be back for a long time.' "

After dinner Nick came back to my place for coffee. "You have a message on your answering machine," he said as I filled the coffeepot.

"Hit the button, will you?" I called as I spooned coffee into the paper filter.

The message was from the center's administrator, Don McCloud, asking me to phone him at home.

I did, still feeling a bit punchy from the margarita.

Don answered the phone. "Sorry to bother you at home, Liz, but I thought you needed to know about this in case you get any media calls. There was a death at the center tonight."

I had a mental image of one of the elderly patients having a heart attack in the waiting room. "Just a minute," I said. "Let me get something to write with." I found a pen and a sheet of paper. "Okay, who died?"

"Gina Lawrence, a therapist in the adult clinic."

I told myself I hadn't heard correctly. "What?"

He repeated it. "Did you know her?" he added gently.

"Yes." I felt my knees buckling. The room began to spin.

"Liz!" Nick's face was inches from mine.

"Liz?" Don McCloud's voice was calling from the phone receiver a few feet away from me on the floor.

Nick took the phone, talked for a few minutes in a low voice. "Yes, I'll tell her," he said finally and hung up.

"Gina's dead," I said.

"Yes, I know." Nick stooped down again, cradled me in a tight hug.

"How?" I said from the confines of his arms, my face buried in his cotton dress shirt.

He released me and moved his face so he could see me. "The janitor found her body in her office, slumped over on her desk. There were needle marks on her arm. They think she died of an overdose."

Chapter Three

I SPENT THE NEXT MORNING DEALING WITH THE MEDIA. A woman from KPRC-TV wanted background information about Gina: how long she'd worked at the center, what her job involved. I gave her the information. "Battered women?" the reporter said in a knowing tone. "Do you think one of the abusive husbands came after her?" I told her she'd have to talk to the police about that. I certainly wasn't going to tell her about Gina's own problems in that area.

The *Chronicle* reporter wasn't interested in Gina's background. After doing some legwork, I was able to tell him what he wanted to know: A janitor had found Gina's body at 7:20 p.m. The adult clinic was open that night, but Gina had had no patients scheduled on her appointment calendar. Yes, a security guard was on duty. No, there was no suicide note. An autopsy would determine the cause of death. I'd be damned if I'd tell that hyper little creep about the needle marks on Gina's arm.

"Call me if you find out anything else," he said and hung up.

I sighed. Usually I did not share the public's low regard for members of the mass media. After all, I was romantically involved with one of those pushy, self-important seekers of the truth. Still, after a morning spent talking to reporters, I was badly in need of caffeine.

I found half the human resources department huddled around the coffeepot, talking about Gina's death. What had I found out, they wanted to know, their faces alight with something disturbingly similar to excitement.

As I filled my red coffee mug, I tried to tell myself that shock manifests itself in many forms. "Emilio Garcia found Gina slumped over her desk at 7:20 and called security right away," I said wearily. "They won't even be sure of the cause of death until after the autopsy."

"I heard that she died of a heroin overdose," Lauren said. "Emilio told me he saw the needle on her desk."

I was never sure if the reason that Lauren always knew the latest center gossip was simply that the coffeepot was in her office. Or maybe she was just the kind of woman—pretty, talkative, barely old enough to vote—whom a large number of people liked to confide in. Probably both.

Lauren looked around the group of women. "You don't think some patient just sneaked up on her and jabbed in the needle, do you?" She glanced at the door, as if expecting some syringe-wielding psychopath to rush in any minute.

"I don't think anyone attacked Gina." Donna Hubbard had come in on the last sentence. She marched to the coffeepot and filled a mug that said, "MBAs Do It More Productively."

No one spoke for a moment. I expected everyone to scatter. Donna tended to have that kind of effect on people.

"What do you mean?" Lauren asked her boss. "You think Gina did it herself?"

Donna shrugged. "It wouldn't surprise me. After all, no one who was working last night saw anyone go in or out of Gina's office until Emilio came in and found her body."

"Which doesn't mean much," I pointed out. "Half the

people on her hallway were seeing clients so their doors would have been closed at least part of the time."

"Missy didn't notice anyone go in," Donna said. "And she could see Gina's office from the reception desk. She said the only person who walked in or out of Gina's office last night was Gina herself."

I'd spent enough time around Donna to know that I couldn't win an argument with her; the woman had a deep-seated need to be right. Still I couldn't let this one go. "Maybe Missy was talking to a client or was in the bathroom when someone walked into Gina's office. I'm sure Missy didn't spend every minute staring at Gina's door."

Donna took a sip of coffee, then sent me her Catherine-the-Great-regarding-the-peasants look. "There are other factors, which I'm not at liberty to discuss, that make suicide a strong possibility." Then, without another glance, she marched out of the room.

What factors? What the hell was she talking about? As much as I'd always disliked working with Donna, a control freak who assumed that no one except herself was competent, I'd never seen her lie. She had to know *something* for her to walk off with that smug look on her face.

Donna's exit seemed to signal the end of her staff's coffee break. I turned to leave too. Lauren stopped me. She looked meaningfully in the direction of the hallway, then she said in a stage whisper, "You know Gina used to have a problem with drugs."

"Who told you that?"

Lauren shook her head. She lifted both hands to push back her shiny black hair, a gesture that reminded me of a TV commercial for hair dye. "I can't disclose that. All I can tell you is that I heard Gina was fired from a job at a drug rehab place because she was using drugs.''

''I don't believe it,'' I said, remembering how vehement Gina had been about drugs and alcohol when she was at my apartment.

Lauren shrugged. ''That's just what I heard.'' Unlike Donna, she did not find it necessary to be agreed with.

''Well, don't repeat it to anyone else.'' I stalked out the door.

The morning did not improve. I'd just gotten back to my office when a police officer showed up, wanting to ask me about Gina.

Homicide Detective Maria Ramirez was a wiry, middle-aged woman with sharp eyes and a palpable air of calmness. Refusing my offer of coffee, she perched on the molded plastic chair next to my desk and asked what I could tell her about Gina. She listened attentively, making occasional notes, when I described Gina's encounter with Todd and told her about my last conversation with Gina.

''Do you know where Mr. Murdock was staying while he was in Houston?''

I shook my head again. ''I don't think Gina knew either. About the only thing I did know about Todd was that he was driving a navy Seville.''

She made a note of that. ''What about this threatening letter you said Ms. Lawrence received? Did she show it to you?''

''No, only told me about it.'' I hesitated, trying to decide if I should mention the letter I had gotten. It seemed almost innocuous now. Telling a police officer about it felt like whining to the school nurse about your scraped knee right after your classmate has been rushed to the hospital with a compound fracture. Still, if Gina had been right and my letter really had been intended for her, it was potentially useful information. I told Investigator Ramirez about it.

She had a skeptical look on her round, weathered face, but she kept her opinions to herself. ''You have that letter here?''

As a matter of fact, I did. Of course it was at the bottom of the large, battered black purse I take everywhere, right underneath a low-fat granola bar and a paperback copy of the latest Jonathan Kellerman novel.

Investigator Ramirez studied it. ''What makes you think this was intended for Ms. Lawrence and not you?''

I explained about our office locations and that Gina's and my notes had said basically the same thing, both messages printed with black marker. How Gina figured that Todd had sent both of them. ''And my note didn't have any name on it; Gina's was addressed to her.'' When I said it out loud, the explanation sounded lame.

The detective handed the letter back to me. ''Keep this. If we find the letter to Ms. Lawrence, we might want to compare fingerprints.''

We studied each other for a moment. ''Anything else you want to tell me?'' she asked.

I wanted to say, Look, find Todd and your case is solved. Forget about Gina's ''state of mind'' during the last few weeks and apprehend her murderer. But Maria Ramirez seemed like a woman who could handle her job quite nicely without my input. ''Nothing else I can think of.''

She studied me with sympathetic brown eyes, a look that reminded me of some of the older social workers I knew, mothers who decided to get their MSWs after their kids were in school. Nice, astute women whose life experience had taught them more than the young hotshots who'd gone to grad school the semester after they'd received their bachelor's degree. ''Someone mentioned that Ms. Lawrence seemed depressed lately,'' she said. ''Did you notice that too?''

I thought about it. ''No, not really.'' With its staff of various mental health experts—psychiatrists, clinical psychologists, psychiatric social workers, art therapists, dance therapists, among others—the mental health center sometimes seemed a hotbed of emotional pulse-taking. Everyone diagnosed everyone else's moods, quirks, and psychopathology—a practice I found so intensely irritating that I'd developed an acute aversion to speculating about anyone's psyche.

The detective looked solemn. ''We're talking about serious clinical depression.''

''I never saw that, and I was around Gina a lot.'' But could I have missed it because that wasn't the kind of thing I looked for? ''She seemed understandably upset about Todd harassing her, but she was calmer than I would have been under the circumstances.''

I narrowed my eyes at the police officer. ''Who said she was clinically depressed?''

She checked her notes. ''A woman who worked with her, Olivia Dickson.'' Olivia was a therapist in the adult clinic, cotherapist with Gina of a couple of groups for battered women.

Investigator Ramirez stood up and smiled. ''Thanks for your help. If you think of anything else, call me.''

I told her I would. I waited until she disappeared down the hall before I headed for the cafeteria. There I bought a mega-size Baby Ruth from a vending machine and returned to my office. I closed my office door, propped up my feet, and devoured the candy bar, washing it down with cold coffee. Only after I had finished every morsel of chocolate did I remind myself that I didn't do this kind of thing anymore.

THE MEMORIAL service for Gina was three days later, at the Southwest Unitarian Church.

I was pleased to see that a substantial number of center staff had opted to spend their lunch hour at the service. We seemed to constitute the largest group of mourners. I also recognized Evelyn Jones, the director of a shelter for battered women where Gina had also worked, sitting next to two women who'd been staying at the shelter last month when I'd gone there to do a story for our newsletter. As I glanced around the room, I saw a few other vaguely familiar faces, women I'd seen walking around the center, probably members of one of Gina's groups.

Nat Ryan, a psychologist from the adult clinic, smiled at me when I sat down next to him. On the opposite side of him Olivia Dickson, the therapist who'd led the battered women's groups with Gina, nodded at me. Olivia was a tall, thin woman with beautiful shoulder-length blond hair and big teeth that made her look a bit rabbity. She was wearing black slacks and a black mohair sweater that made her pale face look ashen. Although I didn't know her very well, there was something about Olivia that always made me feel edgy—perhaps her nervous mannerisms or her palpable air of superiority.

Nat leaned over and whispered in my ear, "They find out who did it yet?"

I shook my head. He wore a spicy-smelling aftershave that lingered after he moved away. I usually disliked perfumery scents on men—a sexist prejudice I knew I should be thoroughly ashamed of—but Nat was one of the few men who could carry it off. A brand-new Ph.D., he was boyishly handsome with twinkling blue eyes, wavy brown hair, and a dimple. Nat worked out at a gym almost every night and had the physique to prove it. The only thing that saved him from being insufferable was his barbed jokes about his own narcissism—a hunk with a sense of humor.

An earnest-looking young man in a white clerical robe walked to the front of the chapel. He introduced himself as Tom Rodham, the church pastor. "I knew Gina Lawrence as the leader of a support group for battered women that met here at the church," he said, looking around the room. "I always thought of her as a brave woman who translated her convictions into action. Gina helped numerous frightened women and touched many of our lives."

He paused. "I know there are others here who would like to share with us their memories of Gina." He smiled encouragingly, the good grade school teacher nudging his class to participate in the discussion.

I watched Evelyn Jones walk to the front of the room. She was a tall, heavyset, black woman, somewhere in her forties, wearing a black knit suit. When she spoke, her voice was deep and resonant, a Barbara Jordan kind of voice that commanded attention.

"I'm Evelyn Jones," she said. "I'm the director of a women's shelter, a place where women come to get away from their abusive husbands or boyfriends. I met Gina Lawrence about five months ago when she stopped at the shelter to talk to me about starting a therapy group for the residents."

Evelyn shook her head. "I told her it would never work.

Most of the women weren't at the shelter long enough to benefit from therapy. And the ones who were had more pressing needs than psychological insights. They were terrified that their man was going to kill them, worried about where they were going to live and how they were going to support themselves and their children. So she could see, I said, that psychotherapy was not high on my priority list right now.''

Evelyn looked from face to face. ''Gina just stood there, staring at me. She said she intended to convince these women that they were not victims. They were *survivors*.'' Evelyn Jones' thick index finger jabbed at the air for emphasis. ''She said that my job—getting them out of the abusive situation to a safe shelter—was only the first step. Her job was going to be to help them start a new life.''

Ms. Jones smiled at the memory. When she spoke again, her voice was soft. ''And Gina did that for a lot of women, abused women, hurting women, women who'd forgotten how to believe in themselves. She convinced them''—the deep voice crescendoing—''that *they were strong*.''

Her voice lowered again, became conversational. ''Sometimes she let them cry on her shoulder, sometimes she kicked ass. But she cared about those women, she *helped* those women, and every one of us is going to miss her.''

Head held high, Evelyn Jones marched back to her seat. Nat leaned over to Olivia and me, whispering, ''Why is it that I feel as if I should leap to my feet, applauding?'' Olivia glared at him.

Several more people spoke briefly. A tired-looking woman with short, dishwater-blond hair who wore blue jeans and a faded burgundy blouse told how she'd phoned

Gina to say that her husband said she couldn't come to the group anymore. To make sure she complied, he'd taken the car and all her money. The woman's soft, high-pitched voice quivered when she said how Gina had told her to pack her bags. ''Gina drove right over in her car and took me to our group. And after that she found me a place to stay in a women's shelter.'' The woman shook her head, fighting tears. ''Nobody else ever stood up for me the way Gina did.''

I barely heard the next speaker, another woman from one of Gina's groups. I could feel the tears trickle down my cheeks, and groped in my purse for a tissue. I turned when I heard a noise behind me, just in time to see Todd Murdock stumble out the door. From the way his shoulders were heaving, he looked as if he were crying. From guilt, I wondered, or just grief?

Finally the service was over. I felt exhausted and achy. Ever since Gina had died, I'd had trouble sleeping. When I finally managed to doze off my sleep was fitful, filled with nightmares. Once I'd dreamed that someone was sneaking up behind me with a big syringe. I woke up just as I turned and saw the needle about to plunge into my shoulder.

On the way back to the mental health center I picked up a vegetable sub and Diet Coke to eat at my desk. I would have loved to go home for a badly needed nap, but there was too much work waiting in my office.

Entering the center from the rear door, I thought the hall seemed unusually empty, almost deserted. Everyone must still be getting back from the service. I had left my office door unlocked, and several people had put notes on my desk: telephone messages written in Lauren's flowery handwriting (my phone calls had been transferred to her office), the manuscript for a journal article that a psychiatrist in the geriatric clinic wanted me to look at, a New England hospital's slick employee magazine that our art therapist thought I'd like to see.

I'd already started returning the phone calls before I saw the other message. It was on the far left corner of my desk, a folded paper on the opposite side from the other notes.

I stopped dialing, set down the receiver. With shaking hands I opened the note. Stared at the page of typing paper with the bold black-marker message. DON'T THINK I'VE FORGOTTEN YOU. YOU'LL PAY FOR WHAT YOU DID.

Chapter Four

I FOUND DETECTIVE RAMIREZ'S CARD AND DIALED THE number. A man with a pleasant baritone answered the phone, said Investigator Ramirez wasn't in right now. Could he help me?

I stared at the neatly printed message from my anonymous correspondent until the letters started to blur. "No, thanks," I said, giving him my name and phone number. "Just have her call me when she gets in."

I had a sudden urge to slam my door and barricade myself in my office. But then it hit me: Whoever had left the note had been here, in my office, sometime within the last two hours. Maybe he—or she—had sat in this very chair, read my messages, chuckled over the contents of my desk.

My hands were shaking as I took a sip of Diet Coke. Who could hate me so much? What had I done that was so terrible? *You'll pay for what you did!*

Of course I had asked myself the same question immediately after I received the first note, but none of the names that came to mind felt right. The most obvious answer was Celia Rogers, a woman I'd helped send to prison for murdering my friend Caroline Marshall and attempting to kill Caroline's eight-year-old son. But Nick had called an acquaintance who worked in the Department of Corrections. Celia was still incarcerated, serving a life sentence; she'd had a minor heart attack a few months earlier. Yes, Celia probably did hate me. It was even conceivable that she had somehow managed to hire someone to deliver the letters. But anonymous notes didn't seem like Celia's style. She wouldn't have bothered with any written threats; she would have just hired a hit man to finish the job.

Who else then? Max, my ex-husband, who, I'd heard, was less than pleased about my relationship with Nick. Max didn't care that I was no longer available, just that he wasn't dating anyone himself. And Max *did* seem like the type to write poison-pen letters. In law school he'd once phoned a professor's home at two, three, and four a.m. the day after the man gave Max a low grade on a test. The only problem was I couldn't imagine Max taking time off from his precious job to personally deliver his messages to my office. He would have mailed the letters.

Another problem. Neither of these people had any connection to Gina. As far as I knew, they hadn't even known her.

I watched a white-haired clerk from the business office stroll down the hallway, carrying a can of Dr. Pepper. The most obvious thing Gina and I had in common was our work. If the same person had sent the letters to both of us, it was very likely that person had something to do with the center.

The phone rang. I jumped. "Liz James." My voice sounded unlike me. Scared.

"Liz, it's Olivia Dickson. I meant to talk to you after the memorial service, but you left right away." Her soft, high-pitched voice made it sound like an accusation.

"What can I do for you, Olivia?"

"Well, I've been sorting through Gina's files and all the stuff in her office." She paused.

"Yes?" I prodded.

Olivia sighed. "The policewoman I talked to, Ms. Ramirez, said I should look for some threatening letter Gina received. She said you knew about it."

"Gina just told me about it." I described the letter. "You see anything like that?"

"No, and, believe me, I've gone through everything at least once." Another long sigh. Who was it who'd commented on Olivia's flair for melodrama?

"Maybe it's in her apartment." It suddenly seemed vitally important that Gina's letter be found, particularly now that I'd received a second message. "If you want me to, I'll go there with you and we could look together. I think her downstairs neighbor has a key."

"Gina's ex-husband already packed up everything in her apartment. He told the landlady that he and Gina were still married, and she let him take all of Gina's stuff. The place is empty. So if it was there, the letter is gone."

Olivia did not sound particularly concerned that it was missing. "There are no other papers I should be looking for, are there?" she asked, her tone sarcastic.

What was her problem? "None that I'm aware of. You didn't find anything suspicious, did you?"

"Suspicious in what way?"

"I don't know. Threatening Gina, or expressing anger."

Olivia gave an unpleasant little laugh. "A whole lot of people were angry with Gina. They didn't necessarily put it in writing."

"Who are you talking about?"

"Oh, about two thirds of the people in her groups. That's

the downside of being a confrontal therapist. Not everyone wanted to change in the way Gina dictated.''

Gina herself had said practically the same thing the night she stayed in my apartment. The night before she died. ''You have anyone specific in mind?''

''Aren't you the little detective?'' Olivia said. ''But the answer is no. Right offhand I can't think of any one person who I think would murder her, though several clients were probably angry enough. Gina had that kind of effect on people.'' She waited for me to comment. When I didn't she added, ''One more thing, Liz. I wouldn't be so sure that Gina even received a threatening letter.''

She was starting to irritate me. ''So why would she tell me that she had?''

Before Olivia could respond I'd provided my own answer: Because I had just told Gina that I'd received an anonymous letter. Maybe she'd just wanted to reassure me. Listen, Liz, that letter was intended for me, not you.

''Who knows why Gina did anything?'' Olivia said, her voice tight and angry. ''All I'm telling you is that she was an incorrigible liar. For Gina the end always justified the means.''

On that happy note, Olivia said she needed to go. She was glad that we'd ''clarified things.''

Clarified what? I thought. If Olivia was right and Gina never had received an anonymous note, that would mean there was no connection between Gina's death and my hate mail. In which case, receiving my letter was probably not a prelude to murder.

But what if Olivia was wrong? Just because she hadn't found the letter to Gina didn't mean that it didn't exist. And I had never seen any evidence that Gina was a liar.

I hesitated, trying to figure out what to do next. Doing nothing always drove me nuts. And sitting here in my office, trying to forget that someone intended to harm me, felt very much like doing nothing.

I looked up a number and picked up the phone. "Evelyn," I said when the familiar deep voice answered. "It's Liz James. I'm wondering if I can come over this afternoon and talk to you."

I PARKED my aging Toyota in front of the unmarked Southwest Women's Shelter, a Victorian house on an unassuming block of thirties-era homes in the Heights. Once a separate town, the Heights was now part of Houston, close to downtown and filled with old homes. The shelter was one of the bigger homes on the block, three stories, with a big front porch that no one ever seemed to sit on.

Throughout the Heights, affluent white-collar types had been buying such houses, spending a fortune renovating them, and then showing them to the public on house tours sponsored each year by various charities.

Unfortunately no one had the money to refinish the shelter's hardwood floors, remodel the large but totally out-of-date kitchen, or even replace the faded cabbage rose wallpaper put up everywhere by some former owner. The place had been bought because it was big and, I'd heard, relatively cheap. The only renovation the board had managed in the seven years of its existence was a top-of-the-line security system installed after the husband of one of the residents had broken in through a window and threatened to shoot his wife if she didn't come back home with him.

I had a sense that unseen eyes were watching me as I

knocked on the front door. I'd had the same sensation the first time I came here. After a minute a female voice behind the door demanded to know my name and what I wanted. When I told her, I heard the dead bolt turn.

A pretty but tired-looking young Hispanic woman held the door open for me. She wore the expression I'd seen on residents' faces the last time I was here: curious but wary. "Evelyn is in her office," the young woman said, pointing to the miniscule office at the foot of the stairs. She glanced nervously down the street before locking the door again and walking away.

Someone was with Evelyn in her office, a heavy woman in blue jeans and a black T-shirt, sitting with her back to the door. From her desk Evelyn spotted me standing in the hallway. She waved, calling that she'd be out in five minutes. I sat down in one of the metal folding chairs lining the hallway.

Two little boys—one around three, the other maybe four or five—came running over to me. "What's your name?" the older one, a skinny and very pale boy with longish auburn hair, asked suspiciously.

I told him. "What's your name?" I asked with a smile.

He didn't answer, just stared at me. "What's *your* name then?" I asked the younger boy, smaller and stockier but with the same red hair. "Are you two brothers?"

The little one, dressed in faded red-and-white-striped Oshkosh B'Gosh coveralls that were a few sizes too big for him, had been standing directly in front of me, inspecting me, his hands on his hips. When I smiled at him, he stepped forward and punched me in the thigh. Hard.

"Hey!" I protested. Both boys darted off. I rubbed my leg where the kid had hit me. It still hurt.

I sighed. My overwhelming impression the last time I was at the shelter was that women needed to be very motivated to get out of their homes to stay in this place. Yes, they were safe here (thanks to the security system and stringent rules forbidding residents to reveal where they were staying). But they also were subject to overcrowding, lack of privacy, the stressed-out behavior of anxious fellow residents and their children, and dozens and dozens of house rules. It wasn't exactly my idea of the place *I'd* want to hide out in.

The woman in Evelyn's office came out, and the little kid who'd punched me ran up to her and grabbed hold of her leg. She seemed not to notice and kept walking.

Standing at the doorway, Evelyn waved me inside. She smiled at me, as if she didn't hear a woman yelling at her kid two feet away, as if Evelyn had all the time in the world to visit with me. "What can I do for you, Liz?"

"Do you remember that story I did about Gina's group? I interviewed several women who were living here."

Evelyn nodded.

"I'm wondering if you could help me to contact those three women." I consulted my notes for the names. "Jean Hill, Chantelle Brown, and Juanita Rodriguez."

"Why?"

Part of me wanted to tell Evelyn about the letters Gina and I had received, to share my suspicion that the residents I'd interviewed—desperate and, in at least one case, visibly angry women—were good candidates for the letter writers. But my common sense told me that Evelyn would want to protect the women. What proof did I have, she'd ask, that they'd done anything? Why should she cause any more stress for three people who were already so overwhelmed?

I fixed my eyes on a spot directly above Evelyn's head. "I'd like to do a follow-up story," I said. "Show how the women are doing two months later, after they've weathered the first crisis."

Evelyn considered it. "I don't know if they'd all want to talk to you again." Particularly, she meant, since at least one of them had been upset about what I'd written about her.

"I'm not going to write about anyone who doesn't want to be interviewed. I just want a chance to talk to them." I fixed Evelyn with a level stare. "Let them decide. Isn't that what everyone is always saying this program is about: the women making their own choices?" It was a cheap shot, and, under other circumstances, I would have been ashamed of myself.

Evelyn rolled her eyes at me: her Get Real look. "Well, Juanita is still at the center. She's moving out soon. You can talk to her. But I'm not sure about Chantelle or Jean. They both left last month. Maybe Jane can tell you how to reach them."

She glanced at her watch. "I need to get moving. I'm already late for a meeting."

I thanked Evelyn, then went to find Jane Holmes, a stocky, gray-haired staff member who'd made a point to tell me that she didn't have much use for the media. I was tempted to tell her that most of the newspaper and television reporters I met didn't view public relations writers as "the media," but I figured she wouldn't be interested.

An anorexic-looking woman with long stringy brown hair told me that she didn't think Jane was working today. Juanita, though, had been in the kitchen a few minutes ago.

Juanita, fortunately, was still there, chopping carrots and

dumping the pieces into a huge stainless steel pot. All the residents were supposed to take turns cooking meals for the group. She glanced up when I walked in. I couldn't tell from her expression whether or not she recognized me.

I reintroduced myself.

She nodded, still chopping carrots. "I remember."

I hesitated. I hate to lie. What I wanted to say was, "Written any good hate mail lately?" Very effective, very smooth. What I said instead was, "I wanted to see how you are doing. I was thinking about doing a short follow-up story."

Juanita didn't react. I remembered now how reserved she'd been when I interviewed her. A self-effacing woman who had married too young, gotten pregnant immediately, and been saddled with a life that quickly spiraled out of her control. It was only when her husband started beating on their four-year-old twin daughters that she decided to take the kids and leave him.

"Evelyn said that you and your kids are going to be moving out soon."

The slight, dark-haired woman nodded. "Tomorrow."

"You've found a job then?" Two months ago she'd been taking a word processing class at the community college.

Juanita stopped chopping and looked at me. "Yes, I work as a secretary at Texas Children's Hospital."

"That's terrific. Congratulations." I remembered that the issues Juanita had been most concerned about—or at least the ones she would admit to—were economic. She, who had only worked in minimum-wage jobs, needed to find some way to support herself and her children.

I edged out on a limb. "I wish Gina were around to hear it. She'd be so happy for you."

Juanita nodded. I thought I glimpsed a look of sadness cross her stoic face. ''Yes.''

She was not a woman given to gushing endorsements, but when I'd talked to her before I thought that, in her quiet way, Juanita liked Gina. And Gina, a gusher, had waxed eloquent about Juanita's hard work and flinty determination to create a better life for her kids.

On a more personal note, I also didn't think Juanita was angry with me. Because of her reticence, my article had hardly mentioned her. Before coming today, I had reread my story. Every quote attributed to Juanita had been unemotional and certainly unobjectionable. In fact, considering the volatility of the topic, what she had said for publication bordered on boring.

''Do you happen to know how I can get in touch with the other women I interviewed—Jean Hill and Chantelle Brown?''

Juanita considered it. ''I think Chantelle said she was moving back to her mother's house in Louisiana. Someplace outside of New Orleans, I think.''

''What about Jean?''

She didn't look at me, just kept chopping. ''She went back to her husband last month.''

On my way out I stopped in the big room at the back of the house. Residents' kids used it as a playroom. I spotted the two boys I'd encountered earlier and made a point to steer clear of them. I generally like children. I'd always pictured myself as a mother of a great brood, but during my marriage I'd had four miscarriages, no babies. For months, years, I'd been depressed about my childlessness. Today, though, seeing those two little hellions, I thought what if my babies had been born and turned out like *that*?

Fortunately I saw some other acquaintances as well. I walked over to the sweet-faced teenaged girl sitting on the floor, playing with a toddler, hoping she'd remember me.

"Hi. You're Elena, right?"

She nodded, smiling. "You wrote the story about the center, didn't you?"

I smiled back. "Yeah, Liz James." I squatted next to her and for a moment we both watched the child bang a plastic dump truck on the floor. I told her about my "follow-up story."

"Juanita's here." Holding the child on her lap, Elena gently removed a handful of her black, curly hair from the boy's fist. She smiled at me. "She really liked the story."

It was the first time I'd heard that. Juanita, I remembered, was a friend of Elena's mother. "I'm glad she did. I already talked to Juanita, though. I'm looking for Chantelle Brown and Jean Hill."

"I don't know about Mrs. Brown. She left right after your story. But that Mrs. Hill." The girl stopped, shook her head, as if censoring whatever she'd been about to say.

"Tell me," I urged. "I won't write what you say."

Elena glanced around the room, checking to see who was in earshot. Only the toddler and a couple of girls playing a noisy board game were close by. "Well, *she* didn't like your story at all. Told everybody at dinner that night that she was going to sue you."

Perversely, the idea amused me. Clearly the woman had overestimated my financial assets. "What else did she say?" Jean Hill had written me to complain about the story, but she hadn't mentioned anything about suing.

"She said you had her saying things she didn't say. She

said when her husband read it, he'd be very angry. He'd hurt her.''

I wanted to retort that Jean had said every word and several much more inflammatory statements that I hadn't included. With an effort, I kept silent. Jean Hill was certainly not the first person to regret shooting off her mouth to a reporter.

''Do you know where Mrs. Hill went when she left here?'' I asked instead.

The slender teenager nodded, but her large brown eyes shifted from my face to the floor. She suddenly seemed transfixed by the orange dump truck.

''What is it? You can tell me, Elena.''

''It's just—'' The girl stopped and seemed to reconsider whatever it was she was about to say.

I waited.

She blurted it out. ''Mrs. Hill went back to her husband. She said it was all your fault. That your story let him know where she was. He called here and told her if she didn't come home, he was going to kill her.''

Chapter Five

By the time I drove back to my office it was almost four-thirty. A really productive workday: first Gina's memorial service, then my visit to the women's shelter, bracketed by announcements that an anonymous correspondent wanted to punish me and a woman I'd interviewed planned to sue me.

Several people were in the mental health center's hallway this time, a gray-haired man and woman walking down the hall and a secretary hurrying into the business office. All the activity should have made me feel better, more confident that a killer wasn't lurking behind my door, but it didn't. I felt my heart thudding wildly as I moved toward my office, afraid of what I'd find there.

I took a deep breath. Walked inside.

There were no unwelcome surprises. No syringe-wielding assailant jumped out at me. No printed threats lay on my desk, only a couple of phone messages in Lauren's handwriting. Unfortunately Detective Ramirez was not one of the callers.

Still feeling edgy, I pulled last month's newsletter from the file and reread my story about the women's shelter. Could Jean Hill's husband really have figured out where she was staying from reading my story? I didn't see how. For one thing, I'd changed her name. In the article Jean was "Anne"—her choice of pseudonym; it was her middle name, she said. Of course Mr. Hill (Jack? John? I remembered Jean had mentioned his name, but I couldn't recall it) might have recognized the situations Jean described and known Anne was someone he knew intimately. Yet I still couldn't understand how he managed to contact Jean. I hadn't listed the name of the shelter or the address. There were no photos with the story. The only identifying fact I'd mentioned was that the shelter was located in the Heights. Maybe I was rationalizing, but unless he was some kind of super-sleuth, I didn't see how Jean's husband could have found her just from reading my article.

I also had a hard time believing that Mr. Hill had even read my story. The newsletter's readership was not (to put it kindly) extensive. The *Center News* was distributed to center employees and volunteers. We had a mailing list that included state legislators and various mental health officials, other social service agencies, and anyone who had ever given the center a donation. There were stacks of newsletters in our waiting rooms, so patients could pick one up too. It was conceivable, I guessed, that Jean Hill's husband had happened to read a copy, but unless he was at the center sometime last month, it didn't seem probable.

I dug through the stack of cassette tapes in my bottom desk drawer until I found one with Jean Hill's name on the label. Usually I didn't bother to tape-record my interviews—I just took notes—but I'd wanted to catch everything the women at the shelter told me, and I thought they might feel inhibited when they saw me jotting down their every word. So instead we'd just talked, and I'd transcribed my notes when I got back to the office. Perhaps if I listened to the tape again, I might figure out why she was so angry with me, or at least find a way to locate her.

The knock on my door startled me. I jumped, dropping the cassette. It bounced off my desk and skidded across the floor.

Todd Murdock stooped and picked it up. He glanced at the label, then handed me the tape. "I need to talk to you," he said, heading, uninvited, toward the plastic chair next to my desk.

I stood there, not sure what to do. I could just walk out. If Todd started after me, I could get help. Someone would page security for me. But the man now sitting next to my desk didn't look dangerous or violent. He had changed his clothes since the memorial service. Dressed in jeans and a white polo shirt, his blond hair windblown, Todd looked less like a slick salesman and more like an aging college student. An unhappy college student.

I settled for the straddler's option: I'd stay and listen to what Todd had to say but be prepared to scream loud enough to make everyone within two hundred feet come running.

"I've been talking to people about Gina," Todd began, not seeming to notice my wariness. "And I don't believe this bullshit that she might have killed herself. Gina is the last person on the face of this earth who would shoot up like that." He made eye contact with me for the first time. His eyes were bloodshot; he looked as if he hadn't slept for a while. "She had this *thing* about drugs."

I nodded. "And alcohol." I hesitated, then decided to tell him what I'd heard about Gina being accused of using drugs on her previous job.

Todd shook his head. "She may have been *accused*," he said, making it sound like a dirty word, "but I'm telling you she didn't do it.'' He ran a hand through his neatly trimmed hair. ''Now if you told me that Gina shot a guy, I would have thought, well, maybe. Gina could be real hot-headed. She wanted things her way and didn't care what she had to do to get it. But what Gina would never do—and no one could make her do—was drink or take drugs. Her dad and sister were alcoholics, and her sister got into drugs too. Not using that stuff was like Gina's religion. I bet we'd still be married if I hadn't started drinking too much beer occasionally.''

Yeah, right. And never mind about the times you beat her up. ''So who do you think killed her?'' I asked.

He shook his head. ''Don't know yet. But I intend to find out.'' He looked at me. ''What I need to get from you is who Gina's enemies were.''

''I don't know of any enemies.'' Although some of her so-called friends didn't seem all that friendly to me lately. ''The only person I ever heard her sound afraid of was you.''

Todd glared at me. ''She didn't have any reason to be. All I wanted to do was talk to her.''

Sure. But what happened when Gina decided she didn't want to listen? The two of us sat there for a minute, scowling at each other. ''Look,'' I finally said, ''I've been trying to think of someone who might have a grudge against her too, but I haven't come up with anyone who had a real motive to kill her.''

''Maybe your idea of a motive and theirs aren't the same thing.''

''True.'' I thought of newspaper stories I'd read. A teenaged boy murdered for his shoes. A woman killed because she flirted with another man. Two teenaged girls raped and beaten to death because they happened to encounter a couple of gang members hell-bent on violence. Maybe I was making the fatal mistake of thinking. What would drive me to murder someone, what affront would so enrage me that I'd snuff out another's life? What if the murderer was already enraged before he even encountered Gina? What if Gina just happened to be at the wrong place at the wrong time, and there was no motive—at least no logical, understandable one—at all?

"One of the last times I talked to her Gina told me she'd had an affair that just ended." Todd's pale blue eyes skewered me with his intensity. "You know who she was having an affair with?"

I shook my head. It was news to me. All the time I'd known Gina I'd never been aware of her being romantically involved with anyone. "How long ago did she tell you that?"

"The morning of the day she died. We talked on the phone. I told her I was leaving town. Had to get back to my business."

Todd was still giving me a narrow-eyed appraisal, as if he thought I was holding out on him about the name of Gina's lover. "Gina said the affair turned sour. Said after our marriage and then this new relationship"—he spat out the word sarcastically—"she'd decided she needed to concentrate all her energy on her work. Screw romance."

He seemed to know a lot more about Gina's life than I did. If he was telling me the truth. I remembered Gina saying Todd thought of her as one of his possessions, like his BMW. Is that what all these questions were about—Todd's jealousy that "his woman" had found someone else?

''My guess is whoever she was sleeping with is her killer,'' Todd said.

''Why do you think that?'' I decided not to mention that he was my prime suspect.

His glibly handsome face darkened. For a few minutes I'd almost forgotten he was a violent man. Now I remembered.

''There was something about Gina.'' Todd was staring off into space. ''She could make you so mad you'd want to kill her. But I loved her too. Really loved her. Gina could be so damn pigheaded, but I never could walk away from her.''

He turned toward me. His face was lined with misery. ''And, believe me, it would have been a lot better for me if I had.''

My phone rang as Todd was walking out the door. He'd get back to me, he said as he left. I wasn't thrilled at the prospect.

I picked up the receiver. ''Liz, this is Maria Ramirez,'' the pleasant, lilting voice said. ''You wanted to talk to me?''

I told the detective about my latest letter.

''Have you shown it to anyone else?'' she asked. ''Has anyone besides you touched it?''

''No, to both questions.'' As I spoke to her I opened my top right desk drawer where I'd put both of the letters.

''I think I'd like to see if we can find any fingerprints besides yours on the letters,'' the detective said.

I opened my second drawer, then the third.

''Oh, shit!''

''What's wrong?'' Detective Ramirez said.

''The letters. I left them in my desk. They're gone.''

Chapter Six

I'D HEARD, OF COURSE, ABOUT THE SENSE OF VIOLATION experienced by people whose homes have been broken into. A friend whose chinchilla (the animal, not the coat) had been stolen from her house told me about her shaking rage and intense fear whenever she walked into the bedroom where her pet had been and imagined strangers gleefully taking something that meant so much to her.

I had a similar sensation when I unlocked my office door the morning after my poison-pen letters disappeared from my desk. Overnight my familiar safe haven had turned into the scene of a crime.

No new messages. Nor had either note returned to my desk drawer. It was almost as if those hateful messages had never arrived. Except I knew they had, and knew too that whoever was playing this cat-and-mouse game with me was counting on my agitation.

Well, screw him. I hoped my correspondent was watching as I grabbed my mug and headed for the coffeepot down the hall. Business as usual. Never mind that I felt as if I'd just been kicked in the stomach. I intended to act as if everything was peachy.

It was harder than I thought it would be. I could barely concentrate on the brochure copy I was writing. I thought I sounded strange, unlike myself, whenever I talked on the phone. It was a relief when, at 9:55, I had to leave to meet a group of high school students who were coming for a tour of the center. I felt paranoid and antisocial when I locked my office door the way Detective Ramirez had advised, but I did it anyway.

Nat Ryan was waiting for me in the auditorium. It was his turn to tell the kids what a therapist does. "You ready for the adolescent onslaught?"

"I'm bracing myself."

The psychology students of Sharpstown High School were a polite, blue-jean-clad group who looked, if not exactly delighted to be here, at least glad to be out of school. I managed to get them all seated, then passed out my brochures and welcomed them to the center. I gave them my three-minute introductory spiel: The mental health center staff saw patients ranging in age from a few months old in the therapeutic nursery to the eighties or nineties in the geriatric clinic. There were special departments for extremely young children, older children, and for adults, older adults, and substance abusers. At another building we had beds for clients who required short-term hospitalization. The center had training programs for psychiatry residents and graduate students in social work, clinical psychology, and child development.

I could see the teenagers were not transfixed by the information. I introduced, "Dr. Nat Ryan, a clinical psychologist who works in our adult clinic," then sat down in the front row.

Nat ambled to the edge of the stage and grinned at the audience. He was wearing corduroy pants and a pale blue turtleneck sweater that nicely displayed his muscular physique. "Ms. James asked me to tell you about my job and the kinds of problems the therapists see in my clinic,'' he said. ''And I'm going to do that. But''—flashing his dimple—''I expect lots of questions. Help me out here.''

Two girls in the row behind me whispered something to each other and giggled.

Nat told the kids how psychotherapists help clients to solve their own problems, why having a caring person listen to you, accept you, and empathize with your pain is therapeutic. He said people didn't have to be really sick to seek out a therapist, they just had to be hurting. With his little anecdotes, funny asides, and good eye contact, Nat made everything he said sound as if he'd thought of it that minute.

I glanced around the auditorium. It was clear that Nat had captured the female vote. Almost every question was from a girl. The last one came from a sultry-voiced brunette in a tight black T-shirt. ''Do you accept any teenage patients?'' she asked, making it sound like a come-on.

Nat treated it like a serious question. ''Clients in my clinic have to be at least eighteen.''

''You don't have any private patients?'' the girl persisted.

Amidst the titters, Nat kept smiling. He looked as if he was enjoying himself. ''No, no private patients.'' He waited a beat, sent the girl an R-rated look. ''Sorry.''

The kids howled. I decided it was time for the tour. Nat winked at me as he walked off the stage. ''Good luck,'' he whispered in my ear. ''I forgot about those raging hormones. Want me to pick up a stick for you to fight them off?''

I didn't need one. Apparently I didn't ooze sex appeal.

When I explained what they were going to see, nobody asked if *I* gave private tours.

We started in the therapeutic nursery. Its central room is a big, carpeted playroom surrounded by offices. Usually several therapists sat cross-legged on the floor playing with toddlers. "Right now there are no clients scheduled," Mary Elton, one of the child therapists, explained to my group. It was the staff's time for conferences.

"I bet you want to know how we do therapy with someone who can't even talk, right?" Mary asked. When a bunch of students nodded, she told them about play therapy.

"But how would anybody know that a baby needs therapy?" asked a reed-thin boy with long hair.

"Usually because he or she is developmentally delayed," Mary said. She was wearing a green pullover sweater that smelled faintly of baby spit. With her graying Afro and warm black eyes, Mary looked like a kindly grandmother—if, that is, your grandmother was into wearing paint-splattered blue jeans. "That means the baby's not doing what he's supposed to be doing at that age."

A tiny girl in the front row raised her hand. "Does that mean that if my little sister isn't talking yet—she's almost two—she should be getting therapy?"

Mary smiled reassuringly. "Not necessarily. Babies do things at different times, the same as other people. It's only if there is some significant delay—maybe a child who's three years old and hasn't said simple words yet—that the child comes here. We like to think that by working with the child early we avert more serious problems later on."

There were a few more questions which Mary answered adeptly. I half-listened, wondering why I was feeling so edgy. It was only when Mary turned to see if I had anything to add that I realized the problem. Without even being aware of it, I'd been watching her, looking for a sign of hidden hostility, any flicker of unexpected emotion when she looked my way. Wondering, could *she* be the person who sent me those letters?

I managed to thank Mary and herd the kids through the remaining stops on the tour. I felt as if I was functioning on autopilot, pretending to be Liz James, PR person, while scoping out my colleagues for signs of subterranean malice.

Get a grip, I scolded myself as I led the group back to their bus. I was turning myself into an emotional wreck for no reason. Not one colleague I'd encountered had inspired a jolt of intuitive suspicion.

I smiled at the teacher who was telling me how much she and the kids had enjoyed seeing the center and waved good-bye to them. I couldn't remember when I'd been so happy to see a group leave.

I deserved a cup of coffee. A couple of jelly doughnuts would be nice too, but I was trying to avoid getting back into bad habits.

Lauren looked up from her desk the minute I headed toward the coffeepot. I noticed she was wearing dangly silver earrings that reached almost to her shoulders. On her they looked good. "You don't have any phone messages," she said. "One guy called, but he didn't want to leave a message or give me his name." She watched me pour coffee. "So how was your tour?"

"Fine." I told her about the teenaged girls' reaction to Nat, expecting she'd be amused.

She wasn't. Lauren's large blue-gray eyes flashed, the corners of her little cupid mouth tightened. "Nat is a very sexy man."

Right. But why get upset about it? Under other circumstances I probably would have been more curious about her reaction. Today, though, I just nodded and poured half a little envelope of Sugar Twin into my mug.

"See you later," I said as I headed for the door.

"Liz." Lauren's alto voice called me back.

I stopped, looked toward her desk.

"You *do* know that Nat and I are going together, don't you?"

"No, I didn't." I wasn't sure what else she wanted me to say: Lucky you! I smiled at her. "He's a nice guy."

Apparently it wasn't the remark she'd hoped for. Lauren's face still looked tense, as if she had a bad toothache. "We are almost engaged."

"Congratulations." I wondered if Nat, who was notorious for going through girlfriends the way others approached a bag of potato chips, thought he was "almost engaged."

"Thanks. I'm real excited. I just wanted to tell somebody. Nat said because we work together we should keep our relationship secret for a while."

Now *that* sounded like Nat. I smiled at her, then glanced pointedly at my watch. "Gee, I'd better get back to my office."

Lauren attempted the kind of dewy-eyed smile appropriate for young, almost-engaged women who are into reading romance novels. It was a toss-up which of us was the lousier actress.

I had lunch with my friend Amanda O'Neil at a deli a few blocks from the center. Over iced tea and a delicious, thick corned beef sandwich that I could almost feel clogging up my arteries, I told Amanda about Lauren and Nat's almost-engagement.

Amanda, as always, was an attentive listener. Although she was a psychologist in the children's clinic, she'd been at the center long enough—fifteen years, even longer than I—to know almost everyone at least casually. In addition, she was a die-hard gossip. Not the malicious type, but the intensely curious variety. Like me.

Amanda raised her elegant eyebrows. She had wonderfully expressive hazel eyes with thick lashes. The rest of her face looked middle-aged, a bit wrinkled and jowly, but the upper third was that of a beauty.

"You're kidding," she said in her melodious contralto.

When I shook my head, she laughed. "Daniel and I saw Nat coming out of the Alley Theatre a couple weeks ago with Olivia Dickson."

"Olivia?" Olivia and Nat had not seemed all that friendly when I'd sat with them at Gina's memorial service. In fact Olivia had seemed distinctly chilly to Nat.

"The two of them were *quite* lovey-dovey." Amanda grinned suddenly. "My boys howl when I use words like that. Nevertheless, you know what I mean. They were so taken with each other they almost ran into me."

"Were they embarrassed that you saw them?"

Amanda considered the question. "Nat wasn't, but Olivia might have been. But then she's always struck me as a very private person, so I didn't think much about it."

"I wonder if he and Olivia broke up or if Nat is seeing both women at the same time."

"It wouldn't surprise me if he were dating both of them. I know he was going out with one of the social work students last summer. She seemed quite besotted with him."

"Besotted?" I repeated as we started walking back to the center. "Now lovey-dovey is one thing . . ."

Amanda shook her head. "No one has any appreciation for my subtle touch with the language. Frankly, Liz, I am disappointed in you."

"Oh, dear," I said sadly.

A too-large chunk of my afternoon was spent in the center conference room at a planning meeting for an upcoming symposium on violence and families. Ironically, Gina was supposed to have been one of the symposium speakers.

Sitting around the big wood table, none of my colleagues seemed especially suspicious. Petty, yes. Cantankerous, territorial, and verbose to boot. But no one seemed to be directing any hostile glances my way or slyly studying me for signs of anxiety. They were too busy arguing about whether we should serve Tex-Mex or a vegetarian menu at the closing night dinner.

I tuned them out and tried to think of some plan of action to catch my anonymous correspondent. Detective Ramirez had warned me to leave the crime-solving to the police. All I was supposed to do was keep my office locked whenever I wasn't in it, never walk alone to my car, keep my eyes and ears open, and call her if I got another letter.

Being careful wasn't enough. Back in my office I closed my door and started checking the phone book for John Hills. Last night I'd listened to the tape of my interview with Jean; she'd called her husband John. Unfortunately there were thirty-eight John Hills in the Houston phone book. Also two Jons, two Jonathans, and seven Johnnies.

I started at the top of the list. Many Hills were not home at four in the afternoon. Sometimes an answering tape gave me the information I needed: a clearly foreign accent, an elderly man, and two perky female voices allowed me to cross a few names off my list. Jean, a thin, intense woman with sharp, angular features, was incapable of perkiness.

I was on John number twenty when a kid answered the phone. A girl with a soft, tentative voice.

"Could I speak to Jean please?" I asked.

"Mom isn't here."

"Could you tell me when you expect her back?" I warned myself not to get excited. There were probably just as many Jean Hills in the area as there were John Hills. Even though it wasn't likely that a lot of Jeans had married Johns, both names were common enough for there to be more than one such couple.

"I don't know," the little girl said. She sounded as if she were crying. "She's been gone for a long time. Do you know where she is?"

Before I could say anything, a man's voice came on the line. "Who is this?" he demanded.

"I was looking for Jean. Can you tell me how I can reach her?"

"Who is this? Why do you need to talk to her?"

I remembered Jean describing her husband: a big, bearded man with wild eyes. He'd broken her jaw with one punch. I hung up. My hand was shaking.

Chapter Seven

From the wary expression on Donna Hubbard's face and her military posture you would have thought I was asking her about her career as an embezzler instead of interviewing her about some minor changes in the center's sick leave policy. "Okay," I said, closing the steno notepad on which I'd been taking notes, "that's all I need to know."

I shuddered to think what would happen if I ever had to interview Donna on some genuinely controversial topic: a sexual harassment case or plans to lay off a significant number of employees—subjects that she, as head of human resources, would be the logical person to go to for official comment. Never mind that Donna's view on what employees had a right to know could be summed up with "as little as possible."

I glanced around her oppressively neat office, at her college diplomas (two of them) on the wall, at her clutter-free desk top, which at this moment held only a leather-bound appointment calendar and a high school graduation picture of Donna's daughter, Jennifer. Sitting behind her desk, Donna looked perfectly in sync with her surroundings: every hair of her frosted hairdo firmly in place, her solid navy suit free of any useless ornamentation.

It crossed my mind that in three days of searching for

colleagues harboring hidden hostility toward me, Donna Hubbard was the one center employee who showed definite distaste for me. Unfortunately, there were two problems with the Donna-as-poison-pen-writer theory. One, Donna didn't like anybody else either. Two, had I committed any grievous wrong to Donna, she was the kind of person who would immediately march into my office to tell me about it. At length. Anonymous hostility was not Donna's style.

I stood up. "Tell Jennifer hi from me the next time you talk to her." I'd become friendly with Donna's then eighteen-year-old daughter two summers ago when she worked at the center.

Something flickered behind the cold gray eyes. Maternal affection perhaps? A stab of loneliness at the thought of her neat, empty house now that her only child was gone? "I'll tell her," Donna said, her expression softening. "Not that Jennifer has much time for her mother now that she's a college girl."

I smiled. "From what I remember of my freshman year, I think that's fairly typical." I paused, thinking of the slender, freckled girl with naturally curly red hair cascading down her back. A bright, shy teenager who, once she started talking, surprised me with her wry humor and her writing talent. By the end of the summer we'd become friends, going to lunch together, chatting at night on the phone. "Why don't you give me Jennifer's phone number? Maybe I'll call her sometime."

"I know Jennifer would enjoy talking to you, but right now she's in the middle of moving. She said the dorm was too noisy to study, so she and two other girls are sharing a rental house near campus. If you remind me next week,

I'll give you the new number,'' she said, glancing at her watch.

My God, wasting time again. The ultimate Donna Hubbard crime. Thinking I'd rather call Austin directory assistance for Jennifer's new number than talk to Donna again, I headed back to my office.

As I neared Lauren's office, two doors down from Donna's, I heard raised voices. Or, more accurately, one voice, Lauren's. ''That is NOT what you said two nights ago when you wanted me to . . .''

Lauren glanced up at that moment and spotted me in the hallway. Red blotches of color spread across her pale face. She marched to the door and slammed it.

But not before I saw who she was yelling at. Nat Ryan, standing next to her desk, looked like a whipped dog.

I wondered, as I unlocked my office door, if true romance was about to hit a snag. Had Lauren just learned about Olivia or another of Nat's girlfriends?

Nat did not look much like a man in love when he stalked down the hall five minutes later. But who said the path to true love was without potholes? Usually he poked his head into my office to chat for a few minutes. Today, however, Nat didn't even glance toward my open door, but just kept walking, eyes straight ahead, face stony. I had a feeling that he and Lauren were no longer ''almost engaged.''

Half an hour later I was trying to figure out the best approach for pitching a story to the *Chronicle* medical reporter when Amanda sauntered into my office. ''Hi,'' she said, perching on the corner of my desk. ''You hear anything more about that family you called the other day, the one whose mother disappeared?''

I shook my head. I'd listened to the tape of my interview with Jean Hill to make sure her husband's name really was John (that was what she called him—"that bastard" or "that son of a bitch John"). But after that I'd done nothing, partly because I wasn't sure what to do. Also partly because (and I wasn't proud of this) the guy on the phone had scared me. Did I want to mess with some explosive potential psychopath when I wasn't even entirely sure that he was the right John Hill?

"Do you think," Amanda said, fixing me with her large hazel eyes, "that maybe we should call back to see how the kids are doing."

It was not a question. Amanda was not just a child psychologist by profession; she was focused—temperamentally, intellectually, instinctively—on kids.

I glanced at my watch. It was 4:10, late enough for the kids to be home from school but too early (I hoped) for their father to be back from work. "Okay," I said, picking up the phone book. "And maybe this time I can find out if this is the Jean Hill I'm looking for."

I waited six rings before a child's voice answered the phone.

"Hi, could I speak to your mother, please?" My voice sounded too hearty, a phony-adult-talking-down-to-a-kid voice.

"She can't come to the phone now," the girl said. "Can I take a message?"

This was not the kid I'd spoken to before. This child sounded older, more savvy.

The problem would be to convince her that I was a benign, harmless stranger who was okay to talk to when her mother wasn't home. "My name is Liz James," I began.

"I'm one of your mom's friends, and I've been trying to reach her."

"She can't come to the phone right now," the kid repeated, apparently not won over by my explanation.

I took a breath. "The last time I called, a couple days ago, your little sister told me that she didn't know where your mother was, that she seemed to have disappeared." I waited for the kid to hang up on me or start yelling that her father had warned her not to talk to me, never, ever.

Instead she started to cry. She seemed to be saying something as she sobbed, but I couldn't understand the words. It sounded as if she was talking to someone at her end of the line.

I covered the mouthpiece. "She's crying."

"Just wait," Amanda said. "She'll talk when she's ready."

It crossed my mind that Amanda would be a lot better at this than I was. Unfortunately, I didn't think it would go over too well to tell the girl, "Hold on a minute. I have somebody here who wants to talk to you."

"It's okay, honey, it's all right," I said while the girl sobbed. But then I thought if the child's mother had actually deserted her, things were very much not okay. So I shut up.

Eventually the child stopped crying. "I don't know where Mommy is," she said in a hoarse voice.

"When did she leave?"

"A week ago. Monday, when we were in school." The girl sounded as if she were going to start crying again.

"I think she's probably going to come back soon," I said with considerably more confidence than I actually felt.

"You do?" The hopefulness in the child's voice broke

my heart. I felt like a shit. Who was I to create rose-colored expectations when I wasn't sure that I'd even met her mother?

"But Daddy says she's not coming home."

"Where does your dad say she's gone?"

"He doesn't know. Mommy doesn't want to be with us anymore." This time the girl couldn't stop the sobs.

"I'm sure that's not true," I said, hoping she was still listening to me. When I interviewed Jean, she had been vehement about protecting her kids from her husband. The woman had been high-strung, but her attachment to her children had seemed unwavering. Knowing that I might be venturing out on a limb, I added, "Honey, maybe your mom doesn't want to be with your daddy anymore, but I know she wants to be with you."

I could hear the girl gulp for breath. "So why did she leave us?"

It was a good question. And one I couldn't answer. "Who's been staying with you kids?" I asked instead. I wasn't sure how many children Jean had; I just knew there was more than one and they were in elementary school.

"No one," she said. "Most nights Daddy doesn't come home until late. Real late when it's dark outside." She sniffled. "Rosie and me get real scared. And hungry too. There's nothing here to eat."

"Are there any neighbors nearby who could help you? Maybe you could go to their house until your dad gets home."

"We don't know anybody. We just moved here. And Daddy said we have to stay in the house." Then she started crying. In earnest.

I covered the mouthpiece and told Amanda what the

child had said. Amanda listened, nodding a few times. I noticed that her eyes had turned steely, her expression grim.

"Tell her," Amanda said, "that we'll come right over and bring them some food."

"What?" Certainly I'd misunderstood her.

Amanda repeated her instructions. "We can't leave two terrified children alone and hungry, can we? Besides I want to see the situation for myself."

I stared at her. In my left ear the older Hill girl—she'd finally told me her name, Emily—still sobbed. "Okay, so we go over there. What if the girls won't let us in? What if their father is home by the time we get there?" I could imagine—vividly—the warm reception we'd get from *him*.

Amanda shrugged, her large eyes registering her impatience. "I don't know. I'll figure that out when we get there."

Chapter Eight

IT WAS ALMOST FIVE-THIRTY BY THE TIME WE FINALLY got to the Hill house, carrying two sacks of McDonald's fare. Amanda also insisted on stopping at a convenience store for some child-approved groceries: peanut butter, jelly, bread, graham crackers, raisins, dry-roasted peanuts.

The Hills, it turned out, lived on one of the more run-down streets on the downtown side of Montrose. Fortunately the drive was only about twenty minutes from the mental health center. I'd had images of Emily saying they lived somewhere near Galveston. I was also afraid that Emily might balk when I told her I was coming over and bringing along a friend. But when I said my friend Amanda and I would be bringing them a meal from the fast-food restaurant of her choice, Emily's only response was, "How long before you get here?"

The Hill home was a small, older frame house set on blocks and badly in need of paint. There was no vehicle in the gravel driveway or under the metal carport.

"I hope *Mr.* Hill doesn't walk in the door when we're sitting in the kitchen talking to his kids," I said to Amanda as we got out of the car. I had a feeling both we and his daughters would regret it if John Hill knew his children had let us into his house.

Amanda sent me her don't-be-a-baby look (an expression

she reserved solely for adults). "I told you," she said, "that I've already talked to my friend at Children's Protective Services. She said if we determine the situation is dangerous to the children, they'll send over someone to investigate."

"I'm sure," I said, "that news will calm down Mr. Hill right away."

I had only knocked once on the metal screen door when it was opened by a skinny, dark-haired girl who was an uncanny miniature version of Jean Hill. She looked nine or maybe ten years old.

"Hi, you're Emily, right? And I bet that's Rosie behind you." I smiled at a small girl with short blond hair who was hungrily eying the McDonald's bags. "I'm Liz and this is my friend Amanda O'Neil."

Amanda smiled her reassuring maternal smile. "Hi, Emily. Hi, Rosie."

Emily appeared uncertain whether or not to let us inside the house. She looked up and down the street, then studied us for a minute with solemn brown eyes. Rosie tugged at the sleeve of Emily's faded turquoise sweatshirt, and finally Emily unlocked the screen door and held it open for us. She checked out the street one more time before slamming the front door shut and locking it.

Rosie, an elfin-faced girl who I guessed was in kindergarten, walked up to Amanda. Wordlessly, with a tentative smile, Rosie took the McDonald's bags. Emily glanced at the grocery sack I was carrying but made no move to take it. "Come on," she said, motioning us to follow her.

The dark rooms that we walked through looked as if they'd been furnished from garage sales or secondhand furniture stores. In the living room a faded flowery chintz chair sat next to a pilly brown and white tweed couch. The harlequin-design curtains at the windows didn't quite reach to the windowsill. But every room we walked through—living room, a room that held only a battered wood desk and chair, kitchen with chipped yellow formica countertops—seemed clean and neat.

Emily led us to the round wooden kitchen table where Rosie was already starting in on her Happy Meal. "You could have waited, Rosie," Emily said, but she was covetously inspecting Rosie's cheeseburger when she said it.

"Sit down and eat," Amanda said. She pulled the chocolate shakes out of the bag, inserted straws, and then placed one in front of each girl. We sat down at the table and watched the children gobble down the food.

They finished every french fry, every bite of cheeseburger, and every last chocolate chip cookie. "Thank you for the meal," Emily said, wiping her face with a paper napkin. She stared significantly at Rosie, jerking her head in our direction.

Rosie dutifully thanked us too. "I love french fries," she added with a satisfied smile.

"Me too," Amanda said, smiling back at her. "Especially those crisp little brown ones."

"Yuck," said Rosie. "They're burned."

Emily sent her younger sister a warning look, but her whole body seemed to relax when Amanda laughed.

"I guess I like them burned," Amanda said, leaning toward the younger sister. "Tell me what else you like, Rosie."

"I like to play with my doll," Rosie said. "Do you want to see her?"

"I'd love to," Amanda said, standing up. "Will you show her to Liz too?"

"Sure," Rosie said, leading us to a tiny bedroom at the back of the house. The room held two twin beds with matching faded pink corduroy bedspreads, an old chest of drawers that someone had painted pale pink, a rag rug between the beds, and a plastic laundry basket that held a few toys.

Emily, looking wary, stood at the doorway while Rosie showed Amanda and me a large baby doll.

"She's beautiful," I said. "What's her name?"

"Melinda," Rosie announced proudly.

"That's a very pretty dress she's wearing," Amanda said, fingering a lavender dress with tiny yellow flowers and a yellow ribbon at the neck.

Rosie's chubby-cheeked face stared up at her. "Mommy made it," she said, her blue eyes filling with tears. "And now Mommy's gone."

Amanda kneeled on the floor close to the sobbing child and then wrapped her arms around the bony frame in the too-large brown corduroy pants and white sweatshirt. Amanda rocked the little girl, crooning something softly into her ear.

From the corner of my eye I saw some movement at the doorway. When I looked up, Emily had disappeared. She returned a minute later, carrying the bag of groceries we'd brought and a plastic stool.

Rosie's sobbing had more or less stopped, though she still sniffled a bit. Amanda had pulled a tissue from her pocket and, smiling gently, was wiping the girl's face. "It's scary, isn't it, when your mom's not here?"

Emily, I noticed, was taking the food out of the bag. I

watched as she opened the bottom bureau drawer and shoved in the jar of peanut butter. The jelly went into the middle drawer, both jars covered with neatly folded clothes.

Emily seemed totally absorbed in her task. When she was through, the box of raisins was buried in her underwear drawer and the graham crackers, bread, and peanuts were at the back of her closet shelf. Emily stepped down from the stool she'd used to reach the closet shelf and, without a word, picked up the stool and walked out of the room.

A minute later she was back in the bedroom, her body practically twitching with tension. "You've got to go now," she told me. "It's 5:45. Daddy might come home any minute."

"No!" Rosie howled, clinging to Amanda. "I don't want them to go!"

Emily turned to her little sister, her face hard. "Don't be stupid, Rosie! You know what he would do to us if he knew we let them in the house."

Rosie didn't answer, only buried her face deeper into Amanda's peach mohair pullover.

Still holding the younger child, Amanda looked squarely at Emily. "What would your dad do to you, Emily, if he found out you let us in?"

Anxiety made the girl's voice shrill. "He'd hit us, that's what. With his black belt. And we'd have to stay in our room all day and not go to school."

"Has he ever done that to you before?" Amanda asked in a quiet voice.

Emily didn't answer, but Rosie pulled at the sleeve of Amanda's sweater. "When we came back from the safe house, we had to stay in our room for two whole days. He put a big lock on the door, and he wouldn't let Mommy see us."

"Please!" Emily grabbed my shoulder. Her thin fingers bit into my skin. "You have to go now!"

Clearly the girl was terrified. I stood up. "Will you two be okay if we leave?" Shouldn't we take the girls with us rather than leave them alone with a monster who didn't feed them and padlocked their bedroom door shut?

"We'll be okay if you *go.*" Emily had darted over to Amanda and was yanking her arm. "Hurry."

Amanda and I looked at each other, then together we moved to the door. When we got to the living room, Emily pushed aside the harlequin curtains and checked out the street. "I don't see him," she said, sounding only mildly relieved.

"Maybe it's one of his late nights," Rosie said, still grasping Amanda's hand.

"We don't *know* that," Emily said fiercely. "Maybe he'll come home early." She walked over to her little sister. For the first time I noticed that she held the McDonald's bags and brown grocery sack, all neatly folded. "Here." She handed the bags to Amanda. "I don't want him to find these." When Amanda took the bags, Emily stooped down to pick up her younger sister. "It's okay, Rosie," she said in a gentler voice. "I'll take care of you."

I hesitated at the door, unwilling to leave them. But Amanda motioned to me with her head and opened the front door. "We'll call you tomorrow," she told Emily.

The door slammed behind us the minute we stepped onto the rickety front porch. But I saw the ugly curtains twitch as we hurried to our car and drove away.

From the passenger seat of Amanda's Honda, I turned

back to see if a car was pulling into the Hill driveway. I didn't see any. "I wanted to take them with us," I said.

"I know," Amanda said. "But legally we can't do that."

"Who cares about *legal*?" I said, remembering the children's grim faces.

Amanda reached over and patted my arm. "First thing tomorrow morning I'll call my friend at CPS. I think she can pull some strings to get a caseworker on this right away."

"Then what?"

"If she sees evidence of abuse, they'll take the kids into protective custody. If the mother doesn't show up, they'll probably put the kids in foster care. They'll also notify the police to try to find out what happened to Mrs. Hill."

We drove in silence for four or five blocks. We turned onto Westheimer, a busy street filled with restaurants and small shops. On the corner of Westheimer and Montrose we saw a car slow down. A young male prostitute, probably no more than seventeen, sidled over to the car and, after thirty seconds of conversation with the driver, got inside.

"But what about tonight?" I asked. "How can we be sure they'll be okay until tomorrow morning?"

Amanda's sigh seemed to fill the dark car. "Pray," she said.

EARLY THE next morning Amanda phoned me at my office. She'd called her friend at CPS, who'd assured Amanda someone would get right on the case. I'd worked in a mental health bureaucracy long enough not to be totally reassured by this news. "Getting right on the case" did not necessarily mean action was imminent. "I'll keep calling her for progress reports," said Amanda, also aware of the problem. We agreed Amanda would phone the children that afternoon after they got home from school. She'd phone me after she talked to them.

I sat staring into my coffee mug after I hung up. I'd spent most of last night worrying about Emily and Rosie, wondering what was happening to them. When had their father shown up? Did he somehow learn—from a slip of Rosie's perhaps, or a comment from a neighbor—that his children had let strangers into his house? And where was Jean? As annoying as I'd found the woman, I couldn't believe she'd voluntarily leave her children with that man.

The light knock on my open office door startled me. I looked up to see Nat Ryan smiling in the doorway. "You have a few minutes to talk?" he asked.

I nodded, waving him in. I wondered if this was to be a professional discussion or if he was going to mention his argument with Lauren that I'd overheard.

Maybe neither. Nat sat down on my comfortable molded plastic guest chair, commenting that he hadn't had a chance to "catch up with me" for a while. I agreed. From there we segued to the topic of a grant proposal Nat was working on with great enthusiasm. Ah, a professional discussion. I mentally prepared myself for a request to edit his proposal.

"I wanted to talk to you about Gina," Nat said, taking me by surprise. He apparently read my reaction because he added, "I heard that you were asking around about some anonymous letter she received."

"Did you see it?" I asked. "Or do you know where it is?"

Nat shook his head. "No, unfortunately, to both questions."

I felt a surge of disappointment. Was he, like Olivia,

going to tell me that Gina had probably fabricated the hate mail?

"What I wanted to tell you," Nat continued, "was that I have a pretty good idea who sent Gina the letter."

I stared at him. "Well, who?" I said when he didn't immediately produce a name.

"Olivia Dickson."

"*Olivia?*" I took a few seconds to take it in. "But why would she do that?" Particularly when she and Gina were working together. Wouldn't they settle their differences, or at least talk about them? (*Share their feelings*, in the self-righteous lingo of my therapist friends.)

"Olivia and Gina were lovers for a while," Nat explained. "Gina was the one who broke it off."

"Gina and Olivia?" I wasn't quite naive enough to expect all of that sexual inclination to wear "Gay Power" sweatshirts, but nevertheless I'd never suspected Gina of being a lesbian. Or Olivia, for that matter.

I squinted at Nat. "Are you sure? The last I'd heard, *you* were going out with Olivia."

"I was," Nat said serenely. "Olivia is bisexual."

Right. Why hadn't *I* thought of that? "And she told you she was having an affair with Gina?"

"The affair was over by then. One night when she'd drunk too many margaritas and was feeling depressed, Olivia told me how Gina had dumped her. Olivia apparently thought everything was fine between them; they were talking about moving in together, and then Gina suddenly announced that their relationship was interfering with her work—she said she needed to have 'a wholehearted commitment to it' or some crap like that—and she wanted to stop seeing so much of Olivia. They could be coworkers and friends, but forget about the romance.''

I remembered what Todd had said about Gina telling him she'd had an affair that had ended badly. I suspected he would be even more surprised than I at the gender of Gina's lover. ''But what makes you think Olivia sent Gina the letter? Couldn't she just tell Gina how upset she was?''

''Oh, she tried to. But, according to Olivia, Gina wasn't very receptive. Which probably means she refused to feel guilty. Also, you know, Gina was never much for talking about her feelings—something Olivia can do for hours on end. Gina was a very action-oriented therapist; she wanted to solve problems, not talk about them ad infinitum. She wanted Olivia to stop bitching and moaning and get on with her life.''

Yes, that was the way Gina would have felt. She had no tolerance for self-pity. ''So did Olivia *tell* you she sent Gina the letter?'' I asked, feeling a bit like a broken record.

Nat shook his handsome head, the expression on his face reminiscent of the cartoon cat who'd just swallowed the canary. ''No, but when I broke up with Olivia, *I* received an anonymous letter. 'Don't think you won't pay for what you did,' something like that. I didn't know that Gina had gotten one too until someone mentioned you'd been looking for it.''

I felt as if my brain was not processing the information fast enough. ''But I received letters too.''

Nat's eyes widened in surprise.

''And I can assure you,'' I added, ''*I* never had an affair with Olivia.''

We studied each other for a moment. Nat shrugged.

"Could be there are two poison-pen writers. Maybe one is a copycat of the other."

"Or maybe someone other than Olivia wrote all of them. Maybe," I added without much conviction, "it was even just a prank."

"Some prank." Nat sighed as he glanced at his watch. "I have a patient coming in five minutes." He waved as he walked out the door.

Chapter Nine

"SO ROSIE AND EMILY ARE OKAY?" I ASKED AMANDA.

Perched on the corner of my desk, the child psychologist nodded. "I only talked to Emily for a few minutes. They were already in Conroe, at their aunt's house—their mother's sister. Emily said she and Rosie were going to share a room with their cousins, Lisa and Katie, who are close to their age."

"I bet they were relieved to get away from their father."

Amanda ran a hand through her kinky hair. "Relieved, and sad, and scared. Emily is afraid her dad is going to make them go back. Terrified that he'll blame them for talking to CPS. And not real sure how she's going to like her new school and having to make new friends."

"What if their dad *does* come to get them?"

"There's a restraining order keeping him away from the girls. He could go to jail if he tries anything."

I remembered what Gina had once said about restraining orders: "I'd hate to know how many women have been killed or injured by a man who was legally restricted from coming anywhere near them." I wanted—badly wanted—to believe the girls were now safe from their father's violence, but I was having a hard time buying my wished-for happy ending. "You said you talked to their aunt. Does *she* know where Jean is?"

Amanda's eyes turned flinty. "Doesn't have a clue. And she said the same thing you did: her sister wouldn't have voluntarily left the kids alone with John. She thinks he killed Jean."

"Oh, God." It's what I had thought too, but I'd hoped I was wrong. "Do you know if the police have questioned him yet?"

"My friend at CPS didn't know. She thought we'd be leaping up and down with joy that she managed to get them out of the house so quickly. They'd had other complaints about Hill too—one from the girls' school—that helped expedite the process. And it was lucky the aunt was willing to take in Rosie and Emily."

I knew Amanda's friend at CPS had a point. For once the bureaucratic wheels had turned quickly. Emily and Rosie were probably more fortunate than a lot of children in similar situations. Nevertheless, I couldn't shake my mental picture of little Rosie clutching her doll, and too-serious Emily, jumping whenever she heard a loud footstep. Both of them wondering why the only parent who'd loved them had suddenly disappeared.

I glanced at my watch: 5:15. "You have time to stop for a drink? I could use a glass of wine right now."

"Sure. Daniel's at a conference in Baltimore. I planned to spend the evening cleaning out my closets." Amanda laughed at my rolled eyes. Our years of friendship had made us tolerant of our differences: To Amanda cleaning, sorting, and throwing away were relaxation while to me they were a prolonged form of torture.

She jumped off my desk. "Let me pick up some things in my office. I'll be back in a minute."

It was more like fifteen minutes before Amanda was

standing in my doorway. "Sorry I took so long. There was a man who was looking for me in the clinic—apparently the father of one of the kids I'm seeing. Unfortunately, no one got his name. We looked all over for him, but he must have left."

"He'll probably phone you tomorrow." I grabbed my purse, switched off the lights, and pulled my office door shut. "Where should we go?"

By the time we got to the parking lot we'd pretty much decided on the bar at the Marriott near the Astrodome. It was reasonably uncrowded and on the way home for both of us.

"Excuse me." A big man stepped from behind a parked car. "I'm wondering if you ladies could help me."

We turned to face him: a huge man with longish brown hair and a scraggly beard, dressed in a flannel shirt and blue jeans. He looked, I thought, like someone who would be cast as a mountain man in a TV western. I glanced around the parking lot for anyone we knew. There was no one.

"I'm looking for Dr. Amanda O'Neil," the man said, pleasantly enough. "Someone inside told me she might be coming out this way."

"She's probably in her office," I said quickly. There was something about the man that made the hairs on the back of my neck stand on end. "If she's not there, you can make an appointment."

Amanda, of course, couldn't let it go at that. Amanda, the Good Samaritan, the earth mother with a Ph.D., had to blurt out, "I'm Amanda O'Neil. How can I help you?"

The man's eyes darted from me to Amanda. Then, apparently deciding that Amanda was the one telling the truth, he took a step toward her. "You've already done enough, Doctor. More than enough. Taken away my girls, for starters."

Oh, shit. Before either of us could move, the man grabbed Amanda.

I screamed.

The man threw Amanda to the ground, then lunged for me.

I jumped, managing to avoid his grasp. John Hill started after me, crouched over, like a wrestler circling his opponent. "*Nobody* messes with my family and gets away with it," he snarled.

I ran between a black Suburban and a white pickup. Heart pounding, I glanced back to see how close he was. And saw what Hill didn't see: Nat Ryan directly behind him.

Nat pinned Hill's arm behind his back and slammed him, face first, into the Suburban. "Now just what the hell's your problem?" Nat demanded.

Hill was taller and a lot heavier than Nat, but Nat's bulk was due to muscle. He was also a good fifteen years younger than Rosie and Emily's father.

"I'm not doing anything," Hill muttered. "I just wanted to talk to her about getting my kids back."

Yeah, right. Talk while blackening an eye. I ran to Amanda, who was limping toward us. "Are you okay?"

"Just a little bruised. You're all right?"

"Yeah, thanks to Nat."

Together we walked to where Nat still had Hill pinned to the car. "Call the police," he told Amanda.

She shook her head. "Not now." She turned to Hill. "I didn't take your girls away from you, Mr. Hill. It was your own behavior—hitting them, locking them in their room—that made CPS remove the children from your home. Beating me or anybody else isn't going to change that."

Amanda's glare would have caused frostbite on a more sensitive type. "I strongly suggest you get some therapeutic help right away and start working on handling your anger more constructively."

I stared at my good friend. Had she lost it altogether? She sounded like some therapist cartoon: lecturing a violent criminal about the need for therapy! "Amanda, I think we should call the police."

Amanda shook her head. "No, Mr. Hill has enough problems. Let him go, Nat."

Still pinning the man's arm, Nat leaned his head close to Hill's ear. "I just want Mr. Hill to realize how lucky he is to get a second chance. But if he ever comes anywhere near you two again, or if I just see him hanging around the parking lot another day, next time he's going to jail. Understand?"

The big man grunted something unintelligible and Nat let him go. Without looking at any of us, Hill headed toward the street.

"I'm sure glad you were here," I told Nat. I didn't like to think what would have happened if he hadn't been.

"Me too." He glanced around the dimly lit parking lot. "I'll walk you to your cars. I want to make sure he's not still lurking around."

The same thought had occurred to me. I was suddenly aware of my heart thudding against my chest. My palms were so sweaty I had to wipe them on my coat. I always had these delayed reactions, as if I needed the extra time to figure out what I was supposed to be feeling. "Uh,

Amanda, let's take one car now and come back later to pick up the other one.''

Nat and Amanda turned to look at me. ''Why don't I just follow you home,'' Nat said. ''It's really not out of my way.''

''I'd appreciate that,'' I said before Amanda could get in a word.

''Why don't you come have a drink with us?'' Amanda said. ''I think we could all use one.''

Nat admitted he would like a beer. John Hill was nowhere in sight as we walked to our respective cars. Nor did he join our three-car mini-caravan to the Marriott.

Perhaps, I told myself half an hour later, after gulping my first frozen margarita, I was overreacting. Amanda, the person Hill had come looking for, appeared calm enough.

''I knew that guy looked familiar.'' Nat set down his beer. ''John Hill, that's right. I didn't recognize him at first because when I saw him he didn't have the beard.''

''Where did you see him?''

''He was a patient.''

''*What?*'' I practically choked on margarita number two.

''It was a court-appointed thing; some judge made him 'seek counseling' after he assaulted his wife—put her in the hospital, if I remember. He came in for one session and never came back. Very uncommunicative. Certainly no motivation to change. His dad beat him and his mother. He felt it was his God-given right to do the same.'' Nat's lip curled. ''A real loser.''

I thought of how often the mental health center's staff had tried to assist the Hill family: John's session with Nat, Jean's participation in Gina and Olivia's battered women's therapy group, Amanda's interceding with Children's Protective Services to get Emily and Rosie away from their father. And now Amanda had refused to report John to the police because she wanted to help him—even if he didn't want to be helped.

"Do you think John would be capable of killing his wife and then hiding the body somewhere?" I asked Nat.

He thought about it for a minute. "I only saw him that once, so I don't have much to base an opinion on. But let's just say that if it turns out he did kill her, I wouldn't be surprised." He caught the expression on my face and grinned. "Yeah, I know. We psychologists are noted for these brilliant, after-the-fact predictions."

I could tell from the stubborn set to her jaw that Amanda was about to launch into a stuffy defense of her profession. I wasn't up to hearing it. "You know, Nat," I said quickly, "I was thinking about our hate mail. You still have that letter?"

He nodded.

"What letter?" Amanda asked.

"Nat got the same kind of letter I did," I explained, then turned back to Nat. "I'd like to see if it has the same handwriting as mine."

"Sure, come look at it. I have it in my files."

Which might explain why his letter wasn't stolen. *He* wasn't dumb enough to leave it at the top of a desk drawer. I told him about Detective Ramirez. "I think we should show her your letter."

Nat hesitated. I knew he was still convinced that Olivia had written the message and probably he didn't want to report her to the police. "Listen, let's talk about it when you come look at my letter. I need to get going. I've got dinner plans."

I wondered if his plans were with Lauren, his almost-fiancée. Had they resolved their differences? Amanda and I thanked him again, and Nat hurried off to his dinner companion.

Fifteen minutes later we decided we needed to leave too. ''Sure you don't want to come home with me? We could pick up some Chinese take-out on the way home,'' I asked Amanda as we walked together to the parking lot. It looked as if it was going to start raining yet again—another day of the damp, muggy weather that seemed to match my edgy mood. ''You know it might not be a bad idea if you spent the night too,'' I added, thinking of Amanda alone in her big house with John Hill still out there looking for her.

''Thanks anyway, but I just want to go home and soak in a hot tub. I'm not even hungry. Guess I ate too many peanuts.'' Amanda leaned over to give me a hug. ''I'm fine, Lizzy. My house has an excellent security system. There's nothing at all to worry about.''

I wanted to believe her. But as I got into my Toyota and quickly locked the doors, I couldn't help remembering Gina's words the last time I'd talked to her: ''Don't worry, Liz. I'm perfectly safe.''

Four hours later Gina was dead.

Chapter Ten

I FELT MY MOOD LIFT THE MINUTE NICK'S CAR STARTED over the causeway connecting Galveston Island to the mainland. Below us sailboats glided by, white sails buoyant. The sun, noticeably absent during the previous week of nonstop rain, now glinted magnificently on the water.

We drove down Broadway Boulevard, with its neat row of palm trees in the esplanade, seeing the restored Victorian houses set high above the ground to protect the contents from flood waters. Although it was only a little over an hour's drive from Houston, Galveston seemed light-years away, a city from another century.

Early in the state's history, Galveston had actually been a bigger and more important city than Houston, but when a man-made ship channel was created connecting inland Houston to the Gulf of Mexico, many of the huge ships that had been docking in Galveston came to Houston instead. Today the city was still a seaport, but most Houstonians viewed it the way I did: a tourist town with great beaches and a good smattering of historical sights for those who got sick of lying in the sun.

"I'm glad you suggested this," I told Nick as we drove by the huge stone Bishop's Palace, complete with gargoyles. Galveston even smelled different: salty, the ocean in the air.

We turned onto Seawall Boulevard. Here the city's charming nineteenth-century aura abruptly stopped. Instead Tourist Town flashed in garish neon lights. This was where the beaches were. In every other available square foot of space were hotels, motels, vacation condominiums, restaurants, and little shops that sold T-shirts, candy bars, and tacky souvenirs.

"What do you want to do first?" Nick was trying hard, I could tell, to be solicitous. In the last weeks things had turned awkward between us. I'd responded to my friend's death and the threats against me by withdrawing, retreating into my shell, and I knew Nick was hurt and confused by my behavior.

I considered the question. I liked checking out the little stores along the cobblestoned Strand historical district and enjoyed being near the water and touring the historical homes. "Let's walk along the beach." It seemed a good place for talking.

Nick pulled into a Wendy's parking lot across from the beach. Ignoring the sign warning that the parking was for customers only, we crossed the street. We waited for a teenaged roller blader to pass us, then descended the steep set of stone stairs to the beach.

The smell of the gulf was less pleasant here, pungent and fishy. I didn't care. For a change the beach wasn't packed with people, the March wind making it too chilly for even die-hard sunbathers. Up ahead of us a father was yelling at two preschool-aged boys who were running back and forth on the stone jetty that jutted into the gulf, but for the most part, we had the place pretty much to ourselves.

"We should get out of town more often," Nick said as we headed down the beach.

"Yeah." I slipped my hand into his. "Maybe we should go away somewhere for the weekend. I haven't been to Austin for a while. Or what about Fredericksburg? Remember those wonderful German bakeries? And the bluebonnets should be in bloom pretty soon. It would be a nice drive."

Nick squeezed my hand. "I was thinking of longer than a weekend, maybe a week or two. A real vacation. We might even try someplace exotic: Hawaii or somewhere in the Caribbean. A guy at work was telling me he got a great package deal to go to Jamaica."

I turned to him, surprised. In the two years we'd been together, I couldn't remember him once leaving the state voluntarily. Now Texas, admittedly, is a very big state. On our last vacation, to Big Bend and Fort Davis, we'd put 1,600 miles on Nick's car. We'd hiked on mountain trails, gone white-water rafting, even stayed a couple nights at a dude ranch. It was a great vacation; I wasn't complaining. I was just stunned that a person who equated lying in the sun with Galveston or Padre Island was suddenly talking about Hawaii. "What brought this on?" I asked. "The Texas chauvinist is suddenly turning cosmopolitan?"

"I just thought it would be nice to get away from all the stress for a while."

It would be nice. Wonderful, in fact. Lying on a beach, drinking a piña colada, my only big decision of the day which trashy novel to read first. I even had some accrued vacation time.

"Maybe," Nick added, "it could be our honeymoon."

I stopped. Directly ahead of me the wild toddler broke free from his father's grasp and zoomed down the stone jetty. He careened to a stop when he realized his racetrack abruptly dropped into the ocean.

I did not know what to say. ''Uh, I'm not so sure about the honeymoon part.''

''Oh.'' Nick let go of my hand. ''I didn't mean to drop it on you that way: Marry me and you get a trip to Hawaii. This isn't the way I intended to propose.''

''It's not that,'' I said, wishing I was somewhere, anywhere else. Wishing I knew what to say. ''You took me by surprise, that's all.''

''You need time to think about it,'' Nick translated.

''Yes. Everything's been so confusing lately. I don't seem to know what I want to do anymore about anything.''

''When do you think you *will* know?''

I knew he was hurt, but the question irritated me. He was pushing me again, pushing me to respond in the way he wanted me to, pushing me to react the way he would. The same thing he'd been doing for these last weeks. Why couldn't he accept the fact that I wasn't like him, that I needed time alone to recover my equilibrium? ''I have no idea,'' I said, more coolly than I intended.

''You trying to say you don't want to marry me?''

''No.'' What was I trying to say? ''I'm just not ready yet to make a decision. I'm sorry. I just need some time.''

Nick had a sick expression on his face, as if I'd punched him in the stomach. ''There's nothing to be sorry about. I guess I'll just have to wait.''

The look on his face broke my heart. We turned and started walking along the beach, the wind nipping at our backs. Neither of us speaking, not bothering to hold hands.

I wondered if he'd asked me earlier, before Gina had died, before I'd started receiving the letters, if I'd have answered differently. Certainly during the last few months I'd begun to suspect that Nick and I would eventually get married. What had happened during the last weeks to change my sense of pleasure at that prospect? Had my feelings about Nick changed? Or was I just temporarily too stressed to focus on romance?

Eventually the cold got to me. "Let's go back to the car. I'm freezing," I told Nick. The sun had disappeared as suddenly as it had emerged, and the wind and my mood chilled me to the bone.

"Sure." Silently we headed back.

We climbed the stone stairs to the sidewalk. Not paying much attention, I started across the street, ahead of Nick.

I looked up just in time to see a blue car heading right at me. If I hadn't jumped backward, the car would have hit me head-on. Instead it missed me by inches, the driver speeding by without a backward glance.

"Liz? Are you okay?" Nick kneeled next to me, his face tense with concern.

I stood up, gingerly shifting my weight onto my foot. Somehow in the process of jumping backward, I'd managed to twist my ankle. "I think so." I glanced at him. "Did you see the driver?"

"Only for a second. Dark-haired woman with glasses. I don't think she even saw you."

I wished I could believe that. "That woman looked exactly like Jean Hill." Jean Hill, who'd left her husband and children, and who blamed me for letting her monstrous husband know where she was hiding the first time she'd tried to escape.

MY ANKLE felt fine on Monday when I went to work. I wished I could have said the same for Nick's and my relationship. We had agreed to table the marriage discussions for a while, but I had a sense that I'd merely managed to postpone a difficult decision.

During the months when my marriage to Max was unraveling I'd come to view my work as a welcome refuge from the messy upheavals of my personal life. As I unlocked my office door Monday morning, I was struck with a sense of loss. Once this had been a place where I felt safe, useful, even loved—part of a community of good, well-meaning people. Now every morning when I switched on the light, I braced myself for some new threat from my anonymous enemy. Today there was no paper with a block-printed message lying on my desk. I sighed, went down the hall to fill my coffee mug, then got to work.

My schedule was filled with meetings, my least favorite kind of day. I'd once mentioned to a psychologist I was interviewing my conviction that nothing substantive ever took place (or at least took place quickly) in a large meeting. His wan, sensitive face scrunched up in discovery: his *aha!* look. "You're an introvert, aren't you?" he said. "One of the differences between an introvert and an extrovert is that the introvert recharges through being alone, while the extrovert does that by being with people. You probably do your most creative thinking alone." I'd managed, with some effort, not to roll my eyes. His insight never made me change my mind about meetings, though after that I kept my opinions to myself.

The only high spot of my day came around four-thirty when Amanda showed up in my office, carrying a spoon and a carton of lemon yogurt. "I only have about fifteen minutes before my next patient," she said, sitting down on my molded plastic chair. "But I wanted to tell you I talked to Emily and Rosie last night. They both seemed in good spirits. Their aunt and uncle had taken them all out for a movie and pizza. I think they've started to think they might like living there after all.''

I watched her spoon yogurt into her mouth. ''What about their dad?''

''Apparently he's not giving them any trouble. The aunt told me John phoned her Thursday, the night he showed up here. She threatened to call the police if he came anywhere near the girls.''

''And he bought that?'' Somehow I couldn't see John Hill being that accommodating. He hadn't struck me as someone who'd give up that easily.

Amanda shrugged. ''It seems too much to hope for, doesn't it? I got the impression the aunt and uncle were pretty realistic people though. They're keeping a close eye on the girls.''

I hoped, for everyone's sake, that John had decided to back off. The thought triggered another, more recent memory. ''Oh, Amanda, you're not going to believe who I thought I saw in Galveston yesterday.''

''Elvis?''

''Jean Hill!'' I told Amanda about the near-collision, watching carefully for her reaction. ''Nick says it was probably just someone who resembled her. Whoever it was, was driving so fast that neither of us really had a good look at her.''

Amanda stared at me. ''But what if it was Jean? It only takes a second—less than a second—to recognize a familiar face.''

I'd spent so much energy trying to talk myself out of it, trying to make myself believe I'd just encountered a reckless driver who probably hadn't even seen me. It was a relief to admit my real belief. "If it was Jean Hill, she was trying to kill me."

"I think you should call that detective you were talking to before." Amanda tossed her empty carton in my wastebasket, then patted my hand. "Be careful," she said.

After she left, I worked for another forty-five minutes, then decided to leave. Nick and I were meeting friends for dinner tonight, and if I hurried home, I'd have time for a quick shower.

I was walking out the door when I remembered I'd told Nat that I'd stop in his office this afternoon to see his hate letter. He said he'd be staying late to work on his grant proposal; I could come any time after five.

I hesitated, wondering if this could wait until tomorrow. But it would probably only take a few minutes, and I did want to see the letter. I started up the stairs to the adult clinic. The light was on in Nat's office, but the door was closed. I knocked.

No one answered. I knocked again.

Karleen Graham, a psychologist whose office was across from Nat's, came down the hall carrying a Burger King bag. "Go on in, Liz," she said. "I know Nat's here. He probably just stepped out for a minute."

Still looking at Karleen, I opened the door. When I turned to walk in, I saw Nat. He was slumped over his desk, his face resting on some papers. What looked like a black garter belt was knotted tightly around his neck.

It was only when people came running to Nat's office that I realized the piercing screams ringing in my ears were coming from me.

Chapter Eleven

I FELT LIKE A BROKEN RECORD: NO, I HADN'T SEEN ANYone or anything unusual before I entered Nat's office. The only person in the hallway was Karleen, whose office was across the hall from Nat's. The third time I described everything I saw when I opened Nat's door I realized how cold I was, how my hands wouldn't stop shaking.

A homicide detective had me go downtown to give my notarized statement at the police station. When that was finished—two and a half hours after I'd discovered Nat's body—I was free to go.

I drove home with the radio blaring some bouncy "soft rock" songs that sounded like elevator music. Usually I would have switched stations, but tonight I was just grateful for noise to distract me. It wasn't until I walked into my apartment that I remembered Nick and our plans for the evening.

I found a bottle of Amaretto, poured myself a glass, and gulped it. I still felt cold. Wrapped in a blanket, I phoned the restaurant and had Nick paged.

"Liz? Where are you?" Nick asked, concern in his voice.

"Home." I took a deep breath. "Nat Ryan was killed today. I found his body."

"My God. You okay?"

I wasn't sure yet. "Yeah, maybe."

"How was he killed?"

"Strangled. With a garter belt."

"You're kidding."

"I wish I were."

Mercifully Nick left it at that. "I'll be right there."

He was knocking at the door ten minutes later. A record. Pappadeux's was usually a twenty-minute drive in good traffic.

"How you doing, sweetheart?" he asked gently, peering down at me with a concerned expression.

I shrugged and finished my Amaretto—my fourth.

"Why don't I get you something to eat?" Nick said. "How 'bout a sandwich and a cup of coffee?"

I suspected he was implying that I'd drunk too much, but I didn't care. I wasn't hungry; I doubted that I would ever be hungry again. All I wanted to do was blot out the image of Nat sprawled across his desk.

It was only after I'd finished two cups of coffee and—at Nick's insistence—a few bites of a ham sandwich that I felt like talking about what had happened. "He looked so . . . *grotesque*, Nick, as if someone hated him so much it wasn't enough to kill him, they wanted to humiliate him too." I wasn't sure that made sense, but suddenly the image of Nat, bug-eyed, that damned garter belt cutting into his neck, was too vivid.

"Nat didn't deserve that," I sobbed. "Who could have done that to him? Who could be so *evil*?"

Nick took me in his arms and let me cry myself out.

Usually crying makes me feel better. That night, though, I just felt drained, empty. And there was something else, something that nagged at me like a throbbing tooth. "You know Nat said he got the same kind of anonymous letter at work that I did. That's why I went to his office—to see it."

Nick's sharp-planed face grew pale. "Are you *sure* it was the same kind of letter?"

"No, I'm not *sure*. When I saw Nat's body, I didn't stop to search his office for the letter."

Nick ignored the sarcasm. "Did Nat tell you what his letter said?"

"It said what mine did: he'd pay for what he did. Didn't specify what he had done either. Nat thought Olivia Dickson sent it to him when he broke up with her. He suspected Olivia also sent the letter to Gina. Apparently Olivia had an affair with Gina too, and Gina dumped her."

Unlike me, Nick did not seem surprised about the news of Gina's sexual preferences. "Can you think of any reasons this Olivia would be angry with you?"

I shook my head. "None that I can think of, unless she was real annoyed that I didn't quote her much in my battered women story; Gina was a lot more quotable, so I used her more. Other than that, I haven't had much contact with Olivia."

"Maybe she was jealous of your friendship with Gina," Nick suggested.

"Why?" Gina and I were friends, but I wouldn't have said we were close friends. "You don't mean she thought *I* was having an affair with Gina, do you?"

Nick shrugged. "She sounds like a possessive, jealous person. Maybe she didn't even think you and Gina were lovers, but she still could have resented the time Gina spent with you."

"She didn't spend a lot of time with me. Gina was so

consumed by her work that she really didn't socialize much with anyone that I know of.''

Nick shook his head. ''That garter belt sounds like a message from a jilted lover. You tell the police about Olivia?''

I felt my face get hot. ''I mentioned the letter—that was the reason I went to Nat's office. But, no, I didn't say anything about Olivia. I guess I didn't want to get her in trouble. I mean, there's no proof that she did anything.''

Nick rolled his eyes. ''Olivia won't go to jail merely because you mention your suspicions. The police will just ask her some questions. And what if Olivia did kill Nat? You want his killer to get away with it?''

I promised I'd phone Detective Ramirez first thing in the morning.

To my relief, Nick decided to spend the night. I fell asleep with his arm wrapped around my waist, comforted by the sound of his snoring.

I dreamed I was running down the dark, empty corridor of the mental health center. Someone was chasing me, laughing maniacally. Getting closer every second. Someone I knew.

I woke up, heart pounding, before whoever-it-was caught me. I sat up in bed, not wanting to go back to sleep, afraid that if I did, my dream would resume where it had left off. Who was it who'd been chasing me? Even now, shivering, grasping my knees to my chest, I thought that laugh—wild, loud, unrestrained—sounded somehow familiar. A deep laugh, perhaps even a crazy one. Who did I know who laughed like that? Or was it just in my dream that I knew my pursuer?

I jumped when Nick reached over and touched my arm.

"What's wrong?" he asked, his voice groggy.

"Just a bad dream. I'm okay. Go back to sleep."

But he didn't. He stretched, then propped his head up with one palm. "What was the dream about?"

"Someone was chasing me at the center. Don't know who." I turned to him. "But that's not the really scary thing. I've just been sitting here thinking that no one saw anyone unusual in the hall by Nat's office. And no one saw anybody around Gina's office the night she died either. Admittedly, there are fewer people around at night, but both times some other employees were nearby."

Nick nodded, sleepy but attentive. "So the killer is inconspicuous. Quick and competent too. He knows what he's doing."

"Yeah, that's probably true." Whoever it was had probably come into the offices, quickly killed his victims, and got out fast. "But what I was thinking about is why no one noticed him entering Gina's and Nat's offices. It seems likely that if there was anyone unfamiliar wandering the halls, someone was likely to see him. People who work at the center notice other people, especially strangers. They're always stopping in the hall to give somebody directions. So the fact that no one spotted anybody unusual must mean that the killer had to be someone they see every day."

It was not the kind of thought designed to lull me to sleep. By the time my alarm rang at 6:45, I'd spent about four hours trying to determine which of my coworkers was so good at murder. I didn't come up with a single satisfactory answer.

BY THE time I got to work at eight, clusters of center employees were already starting to gather in offices, talking in hushed voices of Nat's death. When I went to get coffee, Lauren was sitting sobbing at her desk, saying she couldn't believe this had happened to Nat. Finally even Donna Hubbard took pity on her and told Lauren to go home.

A lot of people stopped in my office to see what I knew. I told them briefly, without any elaboration. The police had told me not to mention the garter belt around Nat's neck, and I didn't. But the fact that fit, muscular Nat Ryan had been killed while sitting in his office was enough to terrify his coworkers. Yes, my colleagues genuinely grieved for Nat, but I could also see the fear in their eyes. If someone was sneaking around killing employees in their offices, who would be the next victim?

I spent much of the morning on the phone with reporters. Most of them already had the basic information (though since no one mentioned a garter belt, I assumed the police had withheld that information). What they wanted from me was background information: what kind of person was Nat, what kind of therapy did he practice, had any patients ever threatened him.

Nat, I said, was a clinical psychologist in the adult clinic who saw a variety of patients. He'd started working at the center three years ago, right after he received his Ph.D. No, I didn't know of any threats from patients or any possible motive for killing Nat. It wasn't clear yet how he'd died; the autopsy would have to determine that.

"Isn't this the second therapist who's died there recently?" asked the *Chronicle* reporter, an aggressive kid with a nasal voice. "What's going on over there?"

"I wish I knew."

"I'd think," he said in a wily voice, "that every therapist in the place would be terrified of being alone in his office."

From the unusual number of mental health professionals I'd just spotted huddled in the lunchroom, he might have had a point. No way, though, was I going to comment on that one. "We are increasing our security. Starting tonight an extra guard will be on duty." Never mind that a security guard had been on the premises on the nights Gina and Nat had been killed.

"Okay," the reporter said after a longish pause, "I guess that's it."

I mentally gave a sigh of relief.

"Oh, just one more question," he said as I was about to hang up. "Who was it who found Ryan's body?"

I took a deep breath, then answered him.

By four-thirty I felt totally exhausted. My night of sleeplessness had caught up with me, and the visible aura of tension throughout the center didn't help either. By midafternoon the halls appeared almost deserted. Even the clients, who were normally walking to and from their appointments, seemed to have suddenly disappeared.

The knock at my door startled me. I looked up from the mail I'd been trying to read to see Detective Ramirez in the doorway.

I'd phoned her in the morning, but she hadn't been in.

"Sorry I didn't get back to you sooner," she said, coming in and sitting down in the chair next to my desk. "I was out working on another case."

She turned her sharp brown eyes on me. She too looked tired. "I heard that you were the one who found Dr. Ryan's body."

I nodded. I told her about the anonymous letter Nat had received, the letter I'd gone to his office to compare to mine. "He told me he thought Olivia Dickson had sent it to him, after he broke off an affair with her.''

The detective listened and made some notes in a small notebook. ''Is this Olivia the same woman I talked to about Gina Lawrence's death?''

''Same one.'' I hesitated for a minute, then added, ''Nat told me that Olivia had had an affair with Gina too. Said that Olivia was very upset when Gina broke it off.''

Investigator Ramirez's face registered no reaction. ''That's interesting. Did many people know about these affairs?''

I shook my head. ''I didn't. At least not about Gina and Olivia.''

The mention of Gina's name reminded me of the question I wanted to ask her. ''By the way, I've been hearing rumors that Gina committed suicide—which I don't believe at all. You aren't considering Gina's death a suicide, are you?''

''No.'' Investigator Ramirez paused, probably considering how much she wanted to tell me. ''There was no evidence of suicide: no note and no fingerprints on the syringe.''

''No fingerprints?''

The detective shook her head, smiling grimly. ''Someone apparently wiped the prints off the syringe. That sure makes it sound as if someone killed her.''

Yes, it sure did. I had to force myself to focus when Investigator Ramirez started to ask me more questions. Did I know of anyone else who might be angry with Nat? Other jilted girlfriends? Any ex-husbands or ex-boyfriends who resented his going out with their former wife or girlfriend?

I said that Lauren was Nat's most recent girlfriend. I wasn't sure whether or not they'd broken up. I also told her about the incident in the parking lot with John Hill, when Nat had come to Amanda's and my rescue. ''Hill seems like a more likely killer to me than Olivia. He's violent and he's a huge guy. I can't imagine skinny Olivia Dickson overpowering Nat, even if she did take him by surprise. Nat was this fitness freak, a bodybuilder.''

''She wouldn't have had to overpower him,'' the detective said. ''The autopsy report came in right before I left. The killer gave him a hard knock on the back of the head before he—or she—twisted that garter belt around his neck. Dr. Ryan died from a skull fracture.''

Chapter Twelve

THE FUNERAL SERVICE FOR NAT RYAN WAS HELD AT A Lutheran church in Bellaire. Nick, to my surprise, insisted on accompanying me. He sat next to me in the dark wooden pew, looking uncharacteristically sedate in a navy suit, white shirt, and burgundy tie, an outfit he wore only for formal occasions.

I glanced around the sanctuary, a high-ceilinged contemporary-looking place with lovely stained glass windows of Jesus, the good shepherd. Several pews ahead of us Lauren, wearing a solid black dress, sat alone, dabbing at her eyes with a wadded tissue. I watched Donna Hubbard stride purposefully down the center aisle, dressed in her navy suit. She nodded at me and then joined Lauren: the human resources contingent.

Directly ahead of us was a group of muscular young men who I assumed were Nat's bodybuilding friends. The guy right ahead of me, a hulking football player type with a blond crew cut, kept glancing around uneasily, either disconcerted by Nat's death or feeling awkward at a funeral.

There was also a group from the adult clinic: Karleen; Olivia; Missy, the clinic receptionist; and a new psychiatric social worker, Dean Somebody-or-Other, who I'd met briefly. A slight man with kinky auburn hair, Dean looked solemn but not especially upset; he probably had hardly known Nat. Karleen and Missy, though, had the glassy-eyed gaze of women in shock. Sitting next to them, Olivia turned and caught my gaze. Her eyes, I saw, before we both glanced away, were red-rimmed and underscored by dark crescents.

I briefly wondered how I looked to anyone scanning the assembled mourners. Were my feelings so clearly reflected on my face? Did I look as tense as I felt? I'd decided not to go to the funeral home the night before to view Nat's body, but my own private images of Nat that last night in his office still flashed into my mind when I least expected them. I'd be driving down Holcombe, thinking about what I was going to eat for dinner when suddenly I'd remember Nat's face, pale and glassy-eyed, the fit body now limp, lifeless.

I turned when a slender, gray-haired woman walked down the aisle, supported by a handsome teenaged boy who had to be Nat's younger brother. I could also see the resemblance to Nat in the woman's wide-set blue eyes and high cheekbones. She'd once been a beautiful woman, probably still was striking when her face was not ravaged by grief. A tall, very pregnant woman with short dark hair, who I assumed was Nat's sister—she had not inherited the other three's blond good looks—held the older woman's other arm. She too looked as if she'd recently been crying. Behind them walked a balding man who was holding the hand of an adorable, apple-cheeked girl, maybe three years old, who was busy looking around the church. When I smiled at her, she waved at me.

Finally a white-robed minister walked to the pulpit. He was a jowly gray-haired man with a deep voice, a grandfatherly man who had obviously known Nat. He told us that Nat had been a lifelong member of this church, a smart, athletic boy who'd helped out at Vacation Bible School and had been especially good with the little kids. Nat had been a sophomore at Stanford University when his father died unexpectedly of a heart attack. After his father's funeral, Nat had insisted on transferring to Rice University so he could be closer to his widowed mother and younger brother and sister.

I half listened as the minister described this paragon of virtues: the devoted son, supportive brother, and doting uncle. A warm, caring man who always had time to listen to a lonely, eighty-year-old parishioner but was still hip enough for the church teenagers to confide in.

A lot of the people sitting around me were crying. In the front row I saw Nat's mother wrap an arm around her younger son's heaving shoulders. Two rows behind them Donna was whispering something to an obviously distraught Lauren.

A woman with a lovely soprano voice began to sing "Abide With Me," accompanied by the church organist. Nick squeezed my hand as I dabbed at my eyes.

Even though I'd been better friends with Gina than Nat, for some reason this service was more upsetting. Perhaps because Nat's flower-covered coffin was lying a few hundred feet away from me. Or because I hadn't had to witness firsthand the grief of Gina's family, or heard what kind of little girl she'd been, what kind of daughter and sister. Gina's memorial service had praised the professional woman; it was more a celebration of her accomplishments than a mourning of her death.

Finally the service was over. Nick and I were making our way to the back of the church when a hand tapped me on the shoulder. I turned to see Lauren. Dressed in her plain black suit, her makeup uncharacteristically muted and eyes red from weeping, she looked as if she'd aged ten years in the last four days. "You *are* going to the house afterward, aren't you?" she asked in a husky voice.

"Your house?" I'd been under the impression that Lauren lived in an apartment.

She shook her head. "Nat's mother's house. It's just a few blocks from here. Charlotte asked me to invite Nat's friends from work."

I told her I was really sorry, but we couldn't make it. Lauren nodded sadly then moved on to extend the invitation to some therapists from the adult clinic.

"She's really the grieving little widow, isn't she?" The voice was unmistakably Olivia's.

I turned to face her. In contrast to Lauren's pale, tear-stained face, Olivia looked flushed, her eyes bright, mouth tight and angry-looking. I ignored her comment and introduced her to Nick.

"Are you a friend of Nat's?" Olivia asked him, sending Nick a critical look.

Nick shook his head. "I just came with Liz. I never met Nat, though he certainly sounded like an impressive guy."

Olivia tossed her long, straight, center-parted hair and snorted disdainfully. "Not quite as impressive as the good reverend would have you believe."

"Oh?" Nick, of course, looked fascinated.

Olivia sent him a sour look. "Believe me, he wasn't such a saint when it came to his relationships with women."

Nick raised an eyebrow. "You one of his girlfriends?"

I thought I saw a flicker of pride in the gray eyes, but perhaps I was imagining it. "A former girlfriend," Olivia said, emphasizing the modifier. "He treated me like shit."

Nick cocked his head to the side, trying, I bet, to look sympathetic. "Really?"

Resisting a strong urge to kick him in the shin, I grabbed Nick's arm. "We really need to get going," I said, sending him a meaningful glance.

Olivia regarded me dolefully. "By the way, since you wanted to play detective when Gina died, I thought I'd let you know my candidate for Nat's murderer."

I stopped tugging on Nick's arm. "Who?"

Olivia's smile was filled with malice. "Lauren." Seeing my reaction, she added, "No, it's not just jealous ravings. Nat dumped Lauren too. He told me they were through, but Lauren just wouldn't accept the fact. She still kept telling everyone that they were engaged a week after Nat told her he wanted to break up."

"That's no proof, though, that she murdered him," I pointed out.

"Maybe not," Olivia conceded, "but it sure is a motive. With Nat dead, Lauren will never have to admit that there wasn't going to be a wedding. She can see this as her great tragic romance—stay in denial for the rest of her life."

I scowled at her. After ten years at the mental health center, it still annoyed me when therapists glibly diagnosed everyone else's psychological problems. And wasn't Olivia the person who'd told Detective Ramirez that Gina was clinically depressed? Apparently everyone—except Olivia, of course—was suffering from serious psychological disorders.

"I bet you were angry at Nat too," Nick said pleasantly.

I expected Olivia to turn on him. Or at least to diagnose his outburst as the act of a sick man with very poor impulse control. Instead she just nodded. "You bet," she said. "But I didn't kill him. As I tell the women in my battered wives groups, the best revenge against some prick who's hurt you is to create a satisfying life for yourself."

But would that have been enough of a revenge for Olivia? Particularly against someone like Nat, who very likely would have been pleased that Olivia was getting on with her life.

Olivia must have sensed my disbelief because she added, "And I *didn't* send any anonymous letters to Nat either. Detective Ramirez asked me about that."

In the rosy light of the church vestibule Olivia's jaw jutted defiantly, her eyes glinted. "I didn't need to write Nat any notes. I'd already told him exactly how I felt about his treatment of me."

Chapter Thirteen

I FOUND OUT ABOUT NICK'S PLAN THE NEXT MORNING. Not, mind you, from Nick himself, but from Lauren of all people. Around ten-thirty, when I was in her office refilling my coffee mug, Lauren mentioned that Nick had just phoned to say he wanted to interview her.

I set down the coffeepot. "Interview you about what?"

Lauren's expression made it clear that she did not share my incredulity. "About Nat," she said in a tone of voice that indicated I was being a little slow.

I studied her through narrowed eyes, taking in her black miniskirt, black silk T-shirt, and black boots: the nineteen-year-old's version of widow's weeds. "Did Nick happen to mention *why* he wanted to interview you about Nat?"

Lauren shrugged. "He's doing some kind of newspaper story about his death, I guess."

I had inferred that much. Clearly Lauren hadn't asked—or cared—what kind of story Nick was planning on writing. Which was possibly why he'd talked to her, instead of me, when he set up the story. I asked Lauren a question she could answer. "When are you having this interview?"

"Today at noon. I'm going to meet him at the Marriott. We'll talk and have lunch at the same time."

How very cozy. Also how sneaky. Did Nick figure he'd have this interview without me even hearing about it? I turned my back to Lauren, dumped Sugar Twin into my coffee and stirred it furiously with a plastic spoon.

I was aware when I glanced up that Lauren was watching me with intense interest. The smirk on her pretty, vacant face made me suspect that Lauren had decided Nick's interview was really an excuse for a date with her. Would that it were so. Nick had once confided in me that the only common denominator among his disparate girlfriends throughout the years was their high IQs.

''Well, let me know how the interview goes,'' I said, trying to sound calm. I suddenly had a nightmarish image of the kind of quotes Nick might get from Lauren, the mental health center's crown princess of gossip. ''Lauren, let me tell you what I tell everyone at the center before their first newspaper interview: Don't tell a reporter anything that you don't want to see in print.''

''Oh, you don't have to worry about me, Liz.'' Lauren smiled sweetly at me.

Somehow I was not reassured. Mug in hand, I marched to my office and dialed Nick's office number. Miraculously he answered his phone.

I got right to the point. ''What the hell do you think you're doing?''

''Uh, could you be a little more specific?'' Nick asked calmly. ''What the hell do I think I'm doing about what?''

I briefly considered slamming down the receiver in his ear, but decided it would be counterproductive. Instead I took a deep breath. ''Why exactly are you interviewing Lauren Jones today? Is that specific enough?''

''Yup.'' There was a brief silence while Nick, I presumed, considered possible answers. Not a good sign.

"I've decided I want to look into the two deaths at your place. Maybe do a couple stories."

"There already have been lots of stories." A fact of which Nick was well aware.

"Not the kind of story I want to do."

I waited. "Which is . . ." I prodded.

"Oh, something in depth. Everything that's been done so far seems pretty superficial."

I translated the BS. "You want to solve the crimes, right? Then do a series of articles about how you did it."

Nick chuckled. "Oh, I don't know that I'd be that grandiose . . ."

Yeah, right. I'd always admired the tiny egos of the investigative reporters I knew. "And exactly when did you plan on telling me about these articles? Reporters, if you forgot, are supposed to go through me, the public relations director, in setting up their interviews."

"Well, I sort of saw talking to Lauren as gathering background information, not a real interview per se."

Before I could get in my scathing retort, Nick said, "Oh, I've got another call on the line. Talk to you later, sweetheart."

Sweetheart? Even though he'd already hung up, I slammed down the phone.

I took five deep breaths, finished my lukewarm coffee, tried to tell myself that I was overreacting, "catastrophizing" as they say in that wonderful mental health bastardization of the English language. But after all my efforts to convince myself otherwise, I still couldn't shake my conviction that Nick's story was going to prove disastrous for the mental health center. My mental health center.

It took less than twenty-four hours for my apprehensions

to be proved correct. During that time Nick got an earful from Lauren and then branched out to other of my colleagues. I did not pick up this information from Nick. I was too angry to even speak to him.

"Who *is* this Nick Finley?" Dr. Seymour Perch, the psychiatrist in charge of the adult clinic, stood in the middle of my office at nine-thirty the next morning, hands on his portly hips. His jowly face was, as usual, expressionless. Only his small, deep-set eyes registered his anger.

"He's a reporter for the *Chronicle*, an investigative reporter." I figured Dr. Perch knew this already, but, if his past behavior was any predictor of present actions, his agenda would be buried under several layers of obfuscation. "I take it that he phoned you. What did he say he wanted?"

Dr. Perch sent me a wary look, as if he had to ask himself whether it was wise to part with this information. He was, I'd been told, a brilliant scientist, the author of dozens of journal articles, but the therapists who worked under him despised him. Cold, inaccessible, and arrogant were some of the nicer adjectives used to describe Perch's management style.

Apparently the good doctor decided it was in his best interest to tell me something about his conversation with Nick. "He said he wanted to interview me about Nat Ryan and Gina Lawrence. He was interested in my insights about them for some kind of in-depth article he's doing." Perch's tone made clear his opinion of a reporter's idea of in-depth analysis.

"And what did you tell him?" I inquired, hoping that Dr. Perch had been as surly, supercilious, and paranoid to Nick as I knew only Seymour could be.

"I told him that I was under the impression that all requests for newspaper interviews were supposed to come through your office.''

Score one for Seymour.

''He said you were aware that he was interested in doing this story.'' Dr. Perch sent me an accusatory glare. Before I could defend myself, he added, ''I also told him that I had no insights into Dr. Ryan and Ms. Lawrence that I wanted to see in print. To which Mr. Finley replied, 'May I quote you on that, Seymour?' ''

I choked back my snicker, shaking my head in mute condemnation of Nick's crass behavior.

''I told Mr. Finley that I would be talking to you about this matter.'' His testy little eyes stared at me, though his voice remained calm. I often wondered if he realized that his eyes always gave him away.

''I think such an article could be very harmful to the institution right now, Liz. There's already been so much adverse publicity about these unfortunate incidents. That certainly is *not* helping our standing in the community. Several board members have already expressed their concern to me about the negative PR.''

Did he actually think he was telling me something I didn't already know? Certainly my own objections to Nick's proposed stories centered on the harm it could do to the center's reputation. A large number of mental health clients do not want to obtain psychotherapy at a murder site. But when I heard my argument expressed by Dr. Perch I realized how cynical it was. Had we already forgotten that two decent, caring professionals had died way before their time?

I nodded. ''I know what you mean. So you refused to be interviewed?''

"Well, no," Perch said. "When I thought about it, I realized that my comments would probably add balance to the story. And, of course, as Mr. Finley pointed out, I *was* Gina's and Nat's department head." Revealing this, Seymour did not even have the grace to look sheepish. "He's coming to interview me at two-thirty."

After lunch Olivia phoned me. "I just talked to your boyfriend. He wanted to know my feelings about Nat and Gina."

I had a mental image of reading Olivia's acerbic observations in the newspaper. "And what did you tell him?"

"I told him that my feelings were none of his goddamned business."

I mentally let out a sigh of relief.

"But then Nick said I could talk to him off-the-record. He promised that nothing I said would appear in print. He needs me to fill him in on who to talk to, to clue him in on the psychological nuances of the situation."

The psychological nuances? I couldn't imagine Nick uttering those words without a sneer. "You already talked to him?"

"Yeah, this morning. I had a patient cancel at the last minute and Nick was able to interview me over the phone. I think I was able to give him some good insights into the case."

"Uh, what kind of insights are we talking about?" I hated to admit, especially to Olivia, how little I knew about this story.

Olivia snorted into the phone. "Why don't you ask him?" she said and hung up.

I tried to, but Nick was not at his desk. Probably right now he was skulking around the center, charming my coworkers into telling him injudicious opinions—which they would blame me for the moment they saw their comments in print.

So what else could I do? I glanced across my desk as I tried to come up with a solution and spotted my ever-present red mug. Yesterday I'd been too proud to pump Lauren for information. I just smiled when she told me how nice Nick was and how sympathetic he'd been about her losing Nat, trying to convince myself that she was a bust as an interview.

Today, though, I needed information. My pride be damned. Grabbing my mug, I marched to Lauren's office.

She smiled when I walked in, obviously glad for an excuse to stop typing. "How you doing, Liz?"

"Okay," I lied. "Lauren, there's something I need to talk to you about." She looked interested. "About the kind of questions Nick asked you during your lunch yesterday."

Lauren looked even more interested. She grinned coyly, tossing her long hair. "He didn't come on to me, if that's what you mean."

"No, that's not what I'm getting at." I tried again. "I'd like to know more about the kind of story Nick is writing." Before she could inquire why I didn't just ask Nick, I added, "He's been kind of vague about what he's looking for."

Lauren nodded knowingly. "Yeah, he thinks your job as a PR person is to prevent him from writing any negative story about the center."

I could feel the tuna salad I'd eaten for lunch rumbling around in my stomach. "He *told* you he planned on writing a negative story?"

Lauren shook her head. She was still dressed in black,

this time a black and white striped mini dress with a white collar. ''He didn't say that exactly. He wants to write a story about who killed Nat and Gina.''

I took a deep breath.

''And he wanted to know who I thought had killed them.''

''What did you say?''

''Olivia.'' Lauren's thin lips twitched. ''Nat told me when he broke up with her she screamed at him that she wanted to kill him. And she was real pissed off at Gina too. Did you know they had this thing going last year? Then Gina dumped her.''

''A lot of people say 'I could kill you' when they're angry,'' I pointed out, ''but they don't really intend to kill anyone.''

Lauren clearly was not convinced by my argument. ''But I *know* Olivia killed Nat,'' she said. ''Nat told me she called that morning to make an appointment to see him at five o'clock.''

I stared at her. And at 5:45, when I'd walked into Nat's office, he was dead.

Chapter Fourteen

By the end of the week I had heard half a dozen complaints about Nick and his interviews. The last and most vocal came from Seymour Perch, who returned to my office Friday morning to tell me that now, after his interview, he had ''serious reservations'' about the kind of story Nick planned on writing.

''What kind of story is that?''

For once Perch's entire face registered his emotion: distaste. ''I'm afraid that Finley sees himself as some kind of journalistic Sherlock Holmes.'' His cold eyes bore into mine. ''I told him he should leave the crime solving to the police. I want you to make sure that he follows that advice.''

I opened my mouth to answer. To point out that I had no control over what Finley did or did not write. What I wanted to say, but didn't have enough guts to, was that if Seymour really wanted to squelch Nick's story he should have sat on his oversized ego and refused to be interviewed.

Perch, however, didn't give me a chance to say boo. He'd issued his orders. Now he stalked out of my office.

''Shithead,'' I muttered maturely to his departing back. I decided what I needed was some coffee. Aided by a jolt of caffeine, I might be able to think more clearly about what I could do about Nick's story.

When, mug in hand, I entered Lauren's office, I saw her huddled with Missy Gould, the receptionist from the adult clinic, the two of them whispering about something. I started to back out the door.

Lauren looked up. "Oh, Liz, you're just the person we need to talk to," she said, waving me into her office. "Missy is upset about the things she told Nick. She's afraid of how they're going to look in print."

Was there anybody who Nick *hadn't* talked to? "Everybody feels that way the first time they're interviewed," I told Missy. "You're always much more critical of what you say than the reader is."

Missy, a plump twenty-year-old with red hair the color of Fergie's, did not look reassured. "It's not that. I mean, I'm not afraid of sounding stupid—though I probably do sound that too. What I'm worried about is getting Emilio in trouble."

"Why would you get him in trouble?" Emilio Garcia was one of the center janitors.

"Well, Mr. Finley asked me if I'd seen anybody in the hallway near Nat's office late that afternoon when he died. I said I really couldn't see the hallway from the reception desk. I had to turn around to see it. Plus we were really busy that afternoon. We always have a lot of patients on Thursday afternoons."

"So how does that get Emilio in trouble?"

Missy's pale cheeks reddened. "I told Mr. Finley that I remembered getting up to go to the bathroom around 4:45 —he's not going to put *that* in the story, is he? And I saw Nat's hallway then. The only one in the hall was Emilio. He was pushing his cleaning cart and was right outside Nat's door."

I shrugged. "So he was cleaning the offices. That's what he's supposed to do."

Missy shook her head, making her long hair tumble over her face. "But he wasn't supposed to be there then. He doesn't usually clean that hall until after everybody leaves at night." She lowered her voice. "That's the thing. Emilio told me he wanted to get off work early that night, and he didn't want his supervisor to know."

"So did Emilio see Nat that afternoon?"

"He said Nat was in a bad mood. He told Emilio not to clean then, to come back after six, because he was going to have an important meeting in his office."

I wondered if the important meeting was his appointment with Olivia at five. When Lauren told me about Olivia's request to see Nat that afternoon she also mentioned that the police had told her Nat had no notations in his appointment calendar for any meetings after three-thirty.

"And besides getting in trouble with his supervisor, Emilio is afraid that everyone will suspect *him* of being the murderer." Missy's blue eyes mirrored her sympathy. "The police have already talked to him a bunch of times. Remember, he was the one who discovered Gina's body. And everybody knows that he and Gina couldn't stand each other."

Apparently I was one of the minority who were unaware of that fact. "How come?" I'd always found Emilio friendly, though sometimes a little too chatty when I was trying to get work done.

"Oh, one time something was taken from Gina's office—I forget what it was—and Gina accused Emilio of taking it when he cleaned her office. It really hurt Emilio's feelings."

Enough to kill her in retaliation? I'd heard of people being killed for sillier motives, but somehow I didn't see Emilio as the killer. Did Nick, I wondered, expect to pull together all these tangled threads to make one coherent story? I was supposed to have dinner later that night with Sherlock Holmes—his attempt to make up with me. I still wasn't sure that I wanted to see him. On the other hand, maybe I'd finally find out what he was writing.

I poured my coffee. "Don't worry," I told Missy on my way out of the office, "I'm sure you didn't get Emilio in trouble."

Her round face brightened. "You know I did see this big, bearded guy in the hall when I came back to my desk. I told Mr. Finley the man looked like a real redneck, somebody you didn't want to run into on a dark street. Maybe he'll write about *him* and not even mention Emilio."

I stared at her. "Did this guy have dark, kind of scraggly hair? Weigh about 250 pounds? Maybe in his late thirties or early forties?"

"Yeah, that's the one," Missy said. "You know him?"

By late afternoon I was still feeling deeply ambivalent about my upcoming dinner with Nick. The way he'd sneaked around me on this story still smarted. Had the man just conveniently forgotten about our so-called relationship—the one supposedly based on mutual trust and respect? I was beginning to suspect that the only thing Nick really cared about was his latest story. Still he'd told me on the phone that he had something important to tell me. What if he had decided to drop the story? Or perhaps he had proof of who the murderer was. Or maybe he just wanted to apologize. Finally I decided I'd eat with him, hear what he had to say, but that I was going to drive myself to the restaurant.

I met Nick at seven-thirty at Hunan Cafe, a small, quiet restaurant where we often ate Chinese food. "You look great," Nick said as he leaned down to kiss me hello. Just as if nothing unusual had transpired between us and our recent heated phone conversations had never taken place. Clearly an apology was not the important thing he wanted to tell me.

"So how was your day?" Nick asked after the waiter had taken our order.

I sent him a frosty look. "Today alone I had three complaints about you and your story. People keep telling me how you're upsetting them."

Nick shrugged. People were always angry with investigative reporters; he was used to it. "I thought I was being exceptionally civil," he said. "That control-freak personnel director of yours—Donna Somebody-or-Other—didn't even want to tell me how long Gina and Nat had worked there, and that arrogant, son of a bitch psychiatrist—a fish name . . . Trout?"

"Perch," I said.

"Yeah, Dr. Perch. *He* wanted to dictate the story to me: his version of events."

He'd piqued my curiosity. "What does he say happened? I heard he was out of town at some psychiatry meeting when Nat died."

"He was. But that's not his story—nothing so tacky as a true-crime story for our board-certified Dr. Seymour. He wants me to write a piece reassuring people that no more violent incidents will be occurring at the center. Steps have been taken to assure employees' and patients' safety."

"You mean the extra security guard at night?"

Nick nodded. "I know all you employees must sleep soundly at night knowing that another exhausted, off-duty cop is somewhere in the building." He took a drink of his beer. "Perch was quite annoyed when I told him that wasn't the way I saw the story. It was only when I was leaving and asked who he thought I should interview for a psychological profile of the killer that he deigned to talk to me again." Nick's grin was not one of a nice person.

"So what kind of person did he say the killer was?"

"Either a psychopath or someone with any one of a number of paranoid disorders that Dr. Perch explained to me at length." Nick rolled his eyes at the memory. In the year we'd been dating, he'd never once swerved from his contempt of psychiatrists and their theories.

"But Perch did say one thing I thought was interesting. He seems to think a patient killed Nat and Gina. He didn't want to admit it, of course. He kept on saying that anything he said would have to be off-the-record."

"Why does he think that?" I interrupted. "About a patient doing it, I mean."

"He seems to think that the killer has some kind of paranoid delusions. I heard a lot about transference, how therapy could trigger some very intense—and possibly sicko—attachments of the patient to his therapist. Perch said it seemed clear that the killer felt very strongly about Gina and Nat. These didn't seem like random killings, but were premeditated, carefully planned out murders. And when I asked if someone who was psychotic would be capable of this much planning, he said paranoid schizophrenics were often capable of logical thinking. They could appear perfectly normal except when you hit the wrong button and ventured into the area of their delusions.''

I chewed a mouthful of spicy Szechuan chicken, thinking over what Nick had said. I swallowed. ''Is Perch thinking that a patient of Nat and Gina killed them? Or is he saying this is some kind of serial killer who had a bad experience in therapy and now wants to knock off all therapists?''

Nick set down his egg roll. ''He seems to think it's not a serial shrink-killer. He's guessing—off-the-record, of course—that the killer is an actual patient of Nat and Gina.''

''One patient?'' When Nick nodded, I added, ''I can't imagine that there are many patients who saw both Gina and Nat. A big percent of the patients Gina saw were battered women, though I guess she saw other clients too.''

''What about Nat? Did he specialize in any group?''

''Not really. He did marital counseling, family therapy, a lot of short-term therapy and groups.''

''So neither of them specialized in paranoid schizophrenia?''

I shook my head. ''If someone was diagnosed as a paranoid schizophrenic, they'd probably be taking medication and be seen in another clinic. The adult clinic handles your garden-variety neuroses, family therapy, marriage counseling, that kind of thing.''

''Could one of the women from Gina's battered women's group have seen Nat for marriage counseling?''

''It's possible, I guess, but not likely. By the time a woman reached Gina, she was usually past the marriage counseling stage. Gina encouraged the abused woman to get out of her marriage, to refuse to believe the husband's assurances that he was going to change.''

"But it's possible that a woman might start out in marriage counseling with Nat and then, realizing it's futile, end up in Gina's battered women's group?"

"Sure. And I could also see some woman regretting her decision to leave a financially comfortable marriage and, needing someone to blame, blaming her therapist. If only Nat had been a better marriage counselor, she and her husband would be living happily ever after. If only Gina hadn't pushed her to leave the jerk, she could afford to buy herself a new dress and continue the kids' piano lessons."

"The husband of a battered woman might also blame the two therapists for her leaving him," Nick said.

"I was thinking the same thing." In fact, I even had a suspect in mind. I told Nick that Missy had said she'd seen a big, bearded man in the hallway outside Nat's office the afternoon he'd died. "And Nat told me he'd seen John Hill, the big, bearded guy who came after Amanda and me in the parking lot, in therapy once."

Nick nodded, but his face did not have the feverish look of anticipation he usually wore when he thought he was on the right track with a story. "But if John Hill was the killer, why did he tie a garter belt around Nat's neck or give Gina a drug overdose? Did he think Nat had been screwing around with his wife? Was his wife using drugs?"

"If Hill really was paranoid—and he sure seemed that way in the parking lot—he could have thought Jean was sleeping with every attractive man she encountered. If he even saw Nat smile at Jean, he could have figured they were lovers. I never heard that Jean was on drugs, but I only saw her a couple of times. She *was* very high-strung, almost hysterical. I guess it was possible she was on something. Maybe Olivia would know." I paused, remembering my delightful phone conversation with Olivia. "I heard you talked to her too."

"Yeah." Nick seemed totally engrossed in spooning rice onto his plate.

"And . . ." I prodded, feeling annoyed.

"She didn't mention that Jean was a drug addict." He sent me a blank look I interpreted as evasion. Finley was devious, but he was not dumb.

"What about her five o'clock meeting with Nat?" I asked.

Nick raised his eyebrows. "So you talked to Lauren too. Olivia claims she never went to Nat's office that day; she called him around four to tell him she needed to move the meeting to another day."

"It's unlikely that she'd admit to being there," I pointed out.

"But there's no proof that she was. No one I talked to saw her go into his office, and one person told me she met Olivia walking to the parking lot a little before five. She said she was going home early because she wasn't feeling well."

"And you believe her?"

"I'm not sure. The fact that Lauren and Olivia so clearly hate each other's guts makes me discount some of the things they're saying."

I tended to feel the same way. "Yeah, Olivia thinks Lauren did it."

Nick nodded wearily. "I know. I only have one problem with that theory. Whoever killed Nat and Gina—assuming they were killed by the same person—planned the murders carefully. I don't see Lauren as being smart enough. Unless, of course, she's a very good actress."

Was she? I'd always thought that Lauren was smarter than she let on, street-smart. "What about Olivia? She's bright enough, and she probably even knew Gina's and Nat's schedules. And because she was a colleague nobody would think anything about her walking in and out of their offices. She even admits to being furious with both of them."

"I know. I thought of all that too. She had motive and opportunity, and she's probably resourceful enough to come up with the heroin and syringe and some kind of club to knock out Nat. Olivia is certainly a possibility, but somehow I don't think she did it."

"How come?"

He grinned. "Too obvious, I guess."

I shook my head. "You read too many mystery novels. I thought, in real life, the obvious person is usually the one who did it."

"What can I say? If it turns out to be Olivia, you can say, 'I told you so.' "

I watched him finish his beer. "By the way, what was the important thing you needed to tell me? Please let it be I've decided to ditch this story."

"Oh, I just thought you'd want to know what I found out this week."

Which, from what I'd just heard, was next to nothing. "So you're still going ahead with the story?"

"Of course I am." He scowled at me. "And you don't have to use that prissy PR voice on me."

My prissy PR voice rose an octave. "I really think this entire story is counterproductive. It's only going to damage the center's reputation even further—maybe keep patients from coming to their appointments because they're afraid of encountering a murderer. A premature story might clue in the murderer that he or she is suspected. Why can't you just let the police solve this?"

Nick's eyes were steely, his jaw clenched. But when he finally spoke, his voice was low and controlled. "You just don't get it, do you? Your life is in danger, Liz, and you just want to pretend that everything is fine. Can't you see that I'm doing this because I'm concerned about you? Damn it, I'm trying to find the killer before he gets to you! And so far the police have *not* solved the case."

"And you think *you* can?" I realized I was practically shouting; the people at the next table turned to stare. I took a deep breath and lowered my voice. "Because I think you're deceiving yourself, Nick. I know your intentions are good, but . . ."

"Bull." Nick's voice was no longer low or controlled. "What you're worried about, Liz, what you're really concerned about, is keeping things nice and peaceful. Never mind that people are dying in their offices, that you yourself have received threats. We don't want to disturb the center big shots or show the world our dirty linen. Let's not rock the boat."

I opened my mouth to protest, but Nick cut me off. "You're so wrapped up in your good-girl routine that you're not even seeing what's going on. It's almost as if you'd rather die than face the fact that somebody hates your guts."

"Go to hell." I threw my napkin on the table and, without another glance at my dinner companion, stalked out of the restaurant.

Chapter Fifteen

I WAS ABOUT FIVE MILES PAST MY FREEWAY EXIT BEfore I thought about where I was going. I'd been so furious with Nick that I just jammed my keys into the ignition and tore out of the restaurant parking lot. I didn't care where I was going just as long as it was far away from Nick Finley and his self-righteous pronouncements. I'd headed for the Southwest Freeway only because it was nearby. And because the speed of my car, the feel of my foot jammed against the accelerator, was a match for my mood.

Good-girl mentality! Afraid to rock the boat! Who the hell did Nick Finley think he was? Contrary to what Nick believed, the problem was not me and my desire to protect the center. The problem was Nick Finley and his swaggering, take-no-prisoners Woodward-and-Bernstein routine. I wanted to find Gina and Nat's murderer as much as he—more than he did, because Gina and Nat were my friends. The difference was that I had enough common sense to know that Nick's bull-in-the-china-shop approach wasn't going to accomplish anything other than breaking some dishes. *I* believed in subtlety, in reason, in carefully putting together the pieces of a crime in the same way you'd assemble a complex jigsaw puzzle. Nick and his pushy, lowbrow attitudes offended me.

I kept driving until I'd worked my way through the first

layers of my anger. Finally, not entirely sure where I was, I exited the freeway and stayed on the feeder road until I saw a street lined with fast-food restaurants. I spotted what I needed: Baskin-Robbins.

Ever since I snapped out of my postdivorce depression, I'd been trying to eliminate my deeply ingrained habit of reaching for chocolate whenever I got upset. Tonight I was losing the battle. Still, wasn't a double scoop of Rocky Road better than a tranquilizer? Or a double Scotch? (On such rationalizations are built the fortunes of Weight Watchers and Jenny Craig.)

I settled into one of the white plastic chairs to eat my ice cream. Delicious ice cream. Creamy, rich, and chocolatey, with little marshmallows and nuts providing an interesting texture. Not for the first time I decided that those apostles of low fat who looked straight into the TV cameras and declared carrot sticks and rice cakes as satisfying a snack as ice cream or potato chips had a screw loose. Or, more likely, they were probably closet binge eaters who furtively gorged on chocolate-covered peanuts at three in the morning.

I finished the last bite of my cone and wiped my hands and face with a paper napkin. I felt better. Not serene, certainly, but less frenzied. The chocolate had calmed me down enough to look at the situation more dispassionately. Clearly my relationship with Nick was on shaky ground. Our latest argument was only one of a dozen situations revealing our diametrically opposite temperaments. I was cautious; Nick was reckless. He acted impulsively; I didn't want to act at all until I'd thought through every angle. I wanted to avoid scenes and confrontations; Nick enjoyed creating them. He thought the adjective abrasive was a compliment; I thought of it as a synonym for scumbag. We both shared an intense curiosity, a quirky idealism, a love of the written word, and a strange sense of humor. But in the too-bright light of the Baskin-Robbins, this did not seem like the basis for an enduring relationship. Probably my hesitation at answering his marriage proposal was because I'd sensed this all along: A marriage between Nick and me would never work out.

I walked to my car, feeling enveloped in a dark cloud of self-pity. The only thing I could recall about the ride home was I didn't have an accident.

The phone was ringing when I walked into my apartment. I considered not answering it, but then decided that if the caller was Nick, he'd keep phoning all night until I finally answered it. "Hello!"

"Was it something that I said?" It was Amanda's contralto, sounding, as always, curious and faintly amused.

"No." I was in no mood to feed her curiosity.

"Ah." Amanda made the syllable sound meaningful. Unlike me in similar situations, she was also willing to let me keep my secrets and move on. "I'm calling to see if you want to come with me tomorrow morning when I drive up to see the Hill girls. I thought I'd take them out to lunch, see how they're doing."

"Sure." Not only would I like to see Emily and Rosie, the prospect of getting out of town was highly appealing. "What time do you want to leave?"

"I'll pick you up around ten." Amanda paused. "And if you decide you want to talk about it, I'll be home all evening."

"Thanks. See you tomorrow." I hung up, feeling edgy.

I turned on my answering machine, poured myself a

glass of white wine, and headed to the bathroom for a long soak in the tub reading Mary Higgins Clark.

When I got out of my bath an hour later my hands and feet were covered with wrinkles, but I hadn't been able to shake my bad mood. I checked my answering tape. No one had phoned. Glad for the refuge of sleep, I went to bed early and slept for eleven hours.

I was ready to go when Amanda arrived the next morning. Also eager to focus on someone else's problems for a while.

"You doing okay?" Amanda asked as we got into her Honda.

"Yeah, fine."

She glanced at me, then turned around to back out the car. "Good."

We drove for a while in companionable silence, heading north on I-10. After spending my childhood with a dogged younger sister who would have been a huge success as a police interrogator, I realized that this was one of the traits I most prized in Amanda: her ability to back off and give me some space.

"You know what I keep thinking about lately?" Amanda asked.

"What?"

"I keep going over what you told me about Nat suspecting Olivia of sending him an anonymous letter. Every time I reach the same conclusion: Olivia just does not strike me as a poison-pen writer."

"Why not? She certainly seems malicious enough."

"I'm not saying she's a saint, just that she seems too temperamental and volatile to go the poison-pen route. I'd expect her to let Gina and Nat know exactly how she felt—

in person. I've seen Olivia at meetings; she isn't at all shy about revealing her displeasure. Now I know this isn't my area of expertise, but I'd think a poison-pen writer would more likely be passive-aggressive, someone who gives you a big grin then goes back to the office to hire a hit man. It seems to me your letter writer is someone who can't—or at least feels he can't—reveal his rage to the person he's angry with."

I tried to think of people who might fit this category. "Like someone who's afraid of losing his job? Or someone who feels powerless and assumes his complaint won't be taken seriously?"

Amanda nodded. "Could be. Or I suppose it might be someone who's just generally secretive. And probably has a streak of sadism too—someone who enjoys seeing his victims squirm."

"What a nice thought, someone watching to see my reaction to his letters." If the letter writer worked at the center, it wouldn't be very difficult to stop by to see if I were glancing over my shoulder every time I walked out of my office, savoring every sign of my nervousness. And I had been nervous.

I tried to remember if anyone had been hanging around more than usual lately, but despite my newfound paranoia no one special came to mind. The problem was that I had the kind of job where people were constantly walking in and out of my office. Any reasonably discreet colleague could easily check on me without me or anyone else noticing.

Fortunately this grim line of thought was cut short by our reaching Conroe.

We cruised down a tree-lined block of small brick houses

that looked as if they'd been built in the forties or fifties, finally finding the address we were looking for at the end of the block. Jean's sister lived in a red brick ranch house, fairly nondescript, except for the profusion of flowers in the front yard. Yellow and white day lilies bordered the house, and vibrant red pansies surrounded the big oak shading the front of the house. Two big clay pots of pink geraniums sat on either side of the front door. Somehow it seemed a good omen. I didn't remember seeing a single shrub or flower at the girls' house.

When we knocked on the front door, a short, dark-haired woman opened the door. She had a lined, pleasant face that had seen too much sun; I guessed she was Jean's older sister. "I bet you're Amanda and Liz," she said with a smile, waving us into her house. "I'm Ann Doggett, Emily and Rosie's aunt. They've been practically crawling the walls waiting for you to get here."

As if on cue, the two little girls emerged from a room at the back of the house. They spotted us and came running. Little Rosie gave Amanda and me big bear hugs, while Emily waited at her aunt's side, smiling shyly.

Both of the girls looked as if they'd gained some much-needed weight. But that wasn't the only change. It took me a minute to figure out what else was different. The kids were relaxed now; even serious Emily seemed to have loosened up. "Staying with you seems to have done wonders for them," I told Ann with a smile.

"I'm working on it. Now do y'all have time for a cup of coffee or a glass of iced tea?"

I glanced at Amanda, who was on the floor talking to Rosie. "Coffee would be nice," she said, "but first Rosie wants us to see her room."

"My room too," Emily said, running ahead to show us the way.

Their bedroom was a big, airy room with two sets of bunk beds, all with matching pink bedspreads. The floor was littered with toys—dolls, Legos, a board game—a pleasant contrast to the stark neatness of the girls' former bedroom.

"That's where I sleep." Rosie pointed to the bottom bunk. "I wanted to sleep on the top, but Aunt Ann said this year the big girls get to sleep on top. Next year I get to."

"No way," said Emily, defending her turf.

After Amanda and I admired their new toys, the girls led us to the kitchen. "Why don't you kids go play in the backyard with Katie and Lisa for a few minutes while we drink our coffee," Ann told her nieces. "We'll come get you in a little bit."

As the door banged shut, Ann poured our coffee, then motioned for us to sit down at her big oak kitchen table. "I read in the paper about that therapist being murdered at your place," she said, taking me by surprise.

"Yes, Nat Ryan," I said, wondering why she was interested. Up close I could see Ann's resemblance to Jean: the same sharp brown eyes, the high cheekbones, though Ann's face was rounder. The differences between them, though, were more noticeable. Jean was a thin, high-strung woman who always seemed on the verge of an anxiety attack. Ann, on the other hand, was calm, plump, and middle-aged frumpy. I wondered if they had looked more like sisters before Jean's life had taken its downhill turn.

Ann nodded. "I'm pretty sure that he was the guy Jean was seeing for marriage counseling."

Amanda and I stared at each other.

"I was under the impression that John was the one who saw Nat for counseling," Amanda said. "Only for one session though."

Ann nodded. "Yeah, John didn't have any use for therapists. He never liked people telling him what to do."

I'd noticed that. "But John agreed to go with Jean for marriage counseling?"

Ann shook her head. "Not John. He refused to go and told Jean not to go back after the first few sessions. He said that Dr. Ryan was giving her bad ideas."

"What kind of bad ideas?"

"Oh, he was telling her basically what I'd been saying for years: leave the bastard, if you'll excuse the language."

"And she took Nat's advice?"

Ann shrugged. "Yeah, she moved out to that women's shelter for a while. I told her she could come here, but Jean said she needed to go someplace where John wouldn't know to look for her. She stopped seeing Dr. Ryan then and started going to a woman therapist. Jean liked Dr. Ryan a lot but didn't have much use for that woman. Said she was too pushy."

A lot of people had said that about Gina. "In men they call it assertive or decisive," Gina used to say, "but in women it's bitchy or overbearing."

I set down my coffee cup. "You know someone saw John outside Dr. Ryan's office on the night he died."

Ann's sharp brown eyes met mine. "That doesn't surprise me one bit. Jean told me that John thought it was all the doctor's fault that she walked out on him." Ann glanced away, her face suddenly bitter. "And as I told the police over and over again, John is a very violent man."

"Has he been giving you any trouble?" Amanda asked.

"He hasn't been here, if that's what you mean. But he phones sometimes, tells me he's going to go to court to get his girls back." Ann's wrinkled face suddenly looked tired. "I keep expecting him to show up one day, grab the girls, and drive away in his car. That's why we never let them play anywhere but the backyard without Jake or me being there."

"That sounds very stressful," Amanda said, leaning across the table to pat Ann's arm.

"Stressful is not the half of it," Ann said, her voice angry. "I told Jean not to marry that man. He was smart, sure, but what good did all his degrees do when he couldn't keep a job? John couldn't get along with anyone. Within six months he was either fired or he quit because of a fight with somebody-or-other."

"What kind of work did he do?" I asked.

"Computers. He was working on a Ph.D. when Jean met him. The man could do anything with computers. If he ever learned to control his temper, he might have made a real good living for his family." Her face contorted with misery. "Instead he probably just used his brain to get away with killing my sister and hiding her body."

"So you feel confident that Jean is dead?" I asked, suddenly remembering the face of the woman in the blue car who'd almost run me over in Galveston. I'd pretty much convinced myself that the driver wasn't Jean, couldn't have been Jean. In the weeks since that incident I'd seen too many other women who looked like Jean Hill but on closer examination were somebody else.

"Sometimes, you know, I have this feeling that Jean is alive. I can just picture her phoning from another state, telling me that she's ready for me to bring the girls to her. But Jake—that's my husband—says that's wishful thinking. That I need to accept the fact that Jean is gone.''

Ann's voice broke into big, gulping sobs.

Chapter Sixteen

LAUREN TURNED WHEN I ENTERED HER OFFICE. "HEY, Liz. How was your weekend?"

I poured my coffee. "Okay, I guess." If you don't want to count breaking up with the man I thought I was in love with. "How was yours?"

"Boring."

I had the sense that Lauren was watching me as I stirred in a spoonful of Cremora and half a packet of Sugar Twin. "Tell me what you did, Liz. Your weekend couldn't have been more boring than mine."

There was something about the way she was talking, her words slow and almost slurred, that made me glance over to inspect her face. Was she drunk? Or stoned? No, certainly not, not at 8:05 on a Monday morning. Something else—a late night or bad night's sleep—must have made her look so out of it. But would simple sleep deprivation make her eyes look so red?

I considered the more innocuous events of my weekend, the for-public-consumption part, and told Lauren briefly about Amanda's and my visit to see the Hill girls. "We took them out to lunch at one of those pizza places with all the kids' games. They really had a ball. It was great to see them happy for a change, acting like little girls instead of miniature-sized grown-ups."

Lauren giggled.

I wasn't sure what was so amusing. I looked at her inquiringly, ready to join in the joke.

"You are such a do-gooder, Liz," Lauren said, shaking her head in a movement that seemed more involuntary than purposeful. Her words now seemed even more slurred. "You know I saw a T-shirt that reminded me of you. Now what did it say again? Oh, yeah, 'It's Great To Always Know What's Best For Everyone.' Isn't that cool?" She laughed again, a mean, stoned laugh.

What was the point in trying to defend myself against someone who tomorrow wouldn't even remember what she'd said? I moved toward the door. And practically ran into Donna Hubbard, who was standing in the doorway.

"I can handle this, Liz," she said coldly.

I, who had been about to leave anyway, felt, absurdly, doubly insulted. First I was called a know-it-all do-gooder, then I was dismissed as a nonentity.

But Donna was not focusing on me or my hurt feelings. Her eyes blazed as she marched to Lauren's desk. "You and I need to have a little talk, miss." Sounding more like the mother of a recalcitrant teenager than a human resources director.

I decided again to leave. As much as Lauren had irritated me, I wouldn't wish the righteous wrath of Donna Hubbard on anyone. Was Donna going to fire her? Lauren was not exactly noted for her stellar work performance, but still I'd always thought Donna had a soft spot for Lauren, maybe because she was so close to her own daughter's age.

I sat at my desk, sipping my coffee and wondering what had gotten into Lauren. Was she taking potshots at everyone today or had I, unknowingly, been annoying her for months? But what had I done? I searched my mind for any do-gooder incidents. In recent weeks I'd listened a lot while Lauren wailed about Nat, how much she missed him, how she didn't know how she'd go on without him. Had I been offering too much unsolicited advice with my sympathy? Did it offend her that I'd said I knew Nat would want her to start getting on with her life?

I glanced up as I heard someone coming down the hall. It was Lauren. Tears were streaming down her face as she ran by. I heard the door to the back parking lot open. So Donna had sent her home.

Squelching any residual do-gooder urges, I remained seated at my desk and started my list of stories for the next newsletter. I was writing a short article about an upcoming symposium for social workers when, out of my peripheral vision, I saw someone walk into my office. I jumped.

"I'm sorry, miss." It was Emilio Garcia, the night janitor, looking embarrassed. "I didn't mean to scare you."

I shook my head. "It's not your fault. I just didn't know you were there, that's all." I smiled at him, waiting for him to tell me whatever he'd come in to say.

He didn't. Not for a good ninety seconds anyway. Instead he looked around my office, as if it was the first time he'd seen it.

"You usually work nights, don't you?" I finally asked. All of my previous encounters with him had always been in the early evening when I was working late to finish some rush project.

He nodded, a short, wiry, dark-haired man in his late fifties. "I still work at night," he said stiffly, as if I'd offended him.

It just wasn't my day.

"I wanted to find out about the story in the newspaper your boyfriend is writing," Emilio said.

"Nick doesn't tell me what he's going to write." And he's not my boyfriend anymore either.

Emilio looked as if this was an occurrence he hadn't anticipated. "I want to know if he's going to write about me, if he's going to say I found Gina's body and was in the hall when Dr. Ryan died."

Gina and Dr. Ryan? Not Gina and Nat or Ms. Lawrence and Dr. Ryan? I wondered if the names reflected his feelings toward the two therapists or if it was just another incidence of generic sexism.

"I really don't know what Nick is going to write," I repeated. "About you or about anyone else. Did you tell him something you don't want printed?" I was probably more likely to get information from Emilio than from Nick.

Then again maybe not. A look of narrow-eyed wariness crossed Emilio's face. "I didn't say nothing to him. I don't like to talk to reporters."

Probably a wise move. "So why do you think Nick will write about you?"

"Missy said she told him she saw me in the hall the night Dr. Ryan died."

"A lot of people were in the hall that night. I was too." When Emilio didn't respond, I added, "Did you, uh, go into Dr. Ryan's office that night?"

Emphatically he shook his head. "He told me to stay out. He had an important meeting."

"Did he say who the meeting was with?"

"No."

The look on his leathery face, the way his dark eyes suddenly darted away from me, told me he was lying. Had

Nat told him who was coming to his office? Or had Emilio seen something—or somebody—in Nat's office that he didn't want to talk about?

"So you didn't see anyone except Nat in his office that night," I persisted.

Emilio looked puzzled. "I talked to him in the hall." He waved his hand, pointing down my hallway. "Not by his office, the other end."

I tried to think what was at the opposite end of Nat's hallway. "By the reception desk, you mean?"

Emilio nodded. "By Olivia's office."

Olivia again! "Had Nat been in Olivia's office?"

Emilio shrugged. "He was in the hall."

It didn't take years of interviewing people to realize this particular line of conversation was leading nowhere. My knee-jerk reaction was to believe Emilio up to a point. Probably he did speak to Nat in the hall outside Olivia's office. But there was something else he knew, something he didn't want to tell me.

I gave it one last shot. "So that was the last time you talked to Nat, outside Olivia's office?"

Emilio seemed fascinated by something on the wall behind me. "Yes, I told you." He moved closer to me. "You tell your boyfriend not to write about me. I don't want no trouble." This time he looked me straight in the eye.

"I don't think you have anything to worry about, Emilio," I said, trying to sound reassuring.

He did not look comforted. Instead his brown eyes grew hard. "You stop your boyfriend." His eyes held mine for a minute, then he turned and stalked out of my office.

I watched him leave. Had it been a threat or was I just imagining it?

Fortunately, I didn't have long to contemplate the question. I had five minutes to get to an interview with two psychiatric social workers who were holding a workshop for stepparents. I grabbed my steno pad and tape recorder, locked my office door, and headed for the children's clinic.

It was a good interview, filled with pithy quotes like, "The new stepparent of a child over eight can never hope to be more than a friendly camp counselor to the child." The two women had a lot of straightforward advice for stressed-out stepparents who found themselves having to deal with a new marriage, a spouse with divided loyalties, and a kid who kept screaming, "You're not my *real* dad."

I walked back to my office thinking of my nine-year-old godchild, Jonathan Marshall, and his relationship with his new stepmother. After a rocky start the two of them seemed to be getting along fine, considerably better, in fact, than Jonathan got along with his father. Take It Slow and Hang In There: Maybe that could be the headline for my story.

I unlocked my office door. As I walked inside I noticed the folded paper on the floor. Someone must have slipped it under my door.

I stooped to pick it up.

The familiar block letters made me feel suddenly nauseous. I dropped the letter on my desk, as if the paper had scorched my fingers.

I forced myself to read the message: GIVE UP. YOU DON'T HAVE WHAT IT TAKES TO OUTSMART ME.

Chapter Seventeen

THE PHONE WAS RINGING AS I WALKED INTO MY OFFICE. I grabbed it on the fourth ring.

"Liz? It's Maria Ramirez."

"Hi." I sat down, bracing myself for the news. This time I'd made sure that no one retrieved my letter. I'd immediately shoved it into a big brown envelope, marched to the parking lot, and locked it in the trunk of my car. After work that day I'd driven downtown and personally handed the envelope to Detective Ramirez.

"The lab tests on your letter came back," she said. "Unfortunately the only fingerprints on the paper were yours."

"And there's no other test that would tell you anything?" I wasn't exactly sure which lab test, but in the age of DNA testing, of crime scene technicians with their sophisticated equipment, couldn't they find some esoteric high-tech test for disclosing the identity of my correspondent?

Detective Ramirez sighed. "Not really. It's cheap typing paper that you could get anywhere."

"Well, at least is it the same kind of printing as in Nat's letter?" Gina's letter, as far as I knew, had never been found.

"We never saw Nat's letter. An officer checked in his file cabinet, but he didn't find anything."

I felt a wave of nausea churning in my stomach. GIVE UP. YOU DON'T HAVE WHAT IT TAKES TO OUTSMART ME.

"Liz, you still there?"

I took a deep breath. "Yeah." I wished I had a handful of saltines, my favorite remedy for morning sickness during my last (and longest) unsuccessful pregnancy.

"You okay?"

"Not really." Not when I thought of what had happened to other recipients of these letters. Not when I contemplated how the writer was still after me and remembered that the police didn't have a single clue as to who my correspondent was.

"We're working on it, Liz." When I didn't respond with reassured noises, the detective went on. "But you know it wouldn't be a bad idea if you took some time off right now, maybe got out of town for a while. Is that a possibility?"

It sounded to me as if she was admitting that she didn't expect to find the killer anytime soon.

The churning in my stomach increased alarmingly. "Sorry, I've got to go." I slammed down the phone and raced to the restroom. I barely made it in time.

Donna Hubbard was in the hallway when I started back to my office. "Are you ill, Liz?" she said, studying my face with a frown. "You certainly don't look good."

I wasn't feeling too great either. "Must be a virus," I lied. "I think I'm going home for the day."

Donna backed away. "Tell Lauren to take your calls."

I paused outside Lauren's office. The scuttlebutt around the center was that Donna had put Lauren on probation. The only times I'd encountered Lauren recently she'd seemed quiet and withdrawn. Neither of us had mentioned her do-gooder crack or why she'd been stoned on a Monday morning. Hadn't, come to think of it, mentioned much of anything else either.

I stuck my head in the open doorway and told Lauren I was leaving for the day.

"I'll take your calls," she said in a flat voice, avoiding eye contact. I noticed she was not wearing black today, but instead had on a long, shapeless beige dress that seemed equally mournful.

I stopped in my office long enough to pick up my purse and cancel an afternoon interview, then locked my door and headed for my car.

I drove to the nearest convenience store, on Holcombe Boulevard, the kind of place where a disproportionate number of Houston's armed robberies seemed to take place. Inside I bought crackers, Seven-Up, and Pepto-Bismol tablets: the full gamut of queasy stomach remedies. I actually was feeling better already: the leave-the-place-where-you're-most-likely-to-be-murdered home remedy, I guessed.

I got back into my car, unsure of what to do next. I wasn't in the mood to spend the day alone in my apartment. I supposed I could go back to work, but I was afraid I'd immediately feel sick again. Of course what I should do, I decided, was go run all the errands I'd been putting off. For instance, I was almost entirely out of groceries; several of the vegetables in the refrigerator bin looked and smelled as if they should be in a science experiment. Still, I hadn't walked out of work to go grocery shopping.

I ended up driving to my sister's house. It was nearby and, if she wasn't volunteering at one of her kids' schools, Margaret could be counted on for sisterly concern.

She came to the door in her leotard, the shocking pink number she wore with matching tights to her Jazzercize class. ''Come on in,'' she said, waving me inside, ''I'm unpacking groceries.''

I followed her to her huge, oak-paneled ''country kitchen'' and sat down at her pine table.

''How come you're not at work?'' Margaret said, as she shoved broccoli and romaine lettuce into her refrigerator.

''Wasn't feeling well. I got another letter at work a couple days ago, and now the police say there are no fingerprints on it and maybe I should go out of town for a while.''

Margaret turned her saucerlike blue eyes on me. ''Why didn't you tell me you got another letter? And what did this one say?''

I ignored the first question and answered the second.

Margaret groaned. She closed the refrigerator door and sat down across from me at the table. ''You want coffee,'' she asked, ''while we work this out?''

I didn't. A year ago, in a wave of self-righteousness, Margaret and her husband Raoul had switched to decaf.

Margaret poured herself a cup and then got down to business. She was a small, solid woman—muscular, not fat—with curly blond hair that sometimes made people who didn't know her dismiss her as an airhead. If they were unlucky enough to act on this assumption, Margaret made sure they soon realized their error. ''You know I've been thinking a lot about the reason someone might be sending you those letters, why anyone would be that angry with you.''

''And what did you come up with?'' Although we disagreed on a vast number of topics, I had a great deal of respect for my sister's intensely logical brain.

Margaret leaned forward. ''Well, I was trying to think of what kind of things usually push people over the edge. Why do average people commit violent acts? And I thought of three things: love, family, and money.''

She was warming to her subject. ''Think about it, Lizzy. Every night on the ten o'clock news there's someone who's shot his ex-wife or her new boyfriend. So what about Nick's ex-wife or his old girlfriends? Maybe your letters aren't connected to those two deaths at all.''

I thought about it. ''Nick's ex-wife is a surgery resident in Chicago. She probably doesn't even know I exist. And the only old girlfriend he ever mentioned seems happily married.''

Still she had said something that intrigued me. ''You know you might be right about the deaths and letters being unconnected,'' I said. ''There might even be two killers. I've just been assuming the deaths were connected because they both took place at the center. But let's say Todd, Gina's ex-husband, killed her. Later when someone else wanted to get rid of Nat—Olivia, for instance, or Lauren—they could do it in his office so it looked as if the same person committed both crimes.''

''And an entirely different person could be writing the letters,'' Margaret agreed. ''The question, of course, is why.''

''I've been wondering that myself.''

Margaret ignored me. ''So let's say it's not one of Nick's ex-girlfriends, though I think I might pursue the subject with him if I were you.'' She sent me the pointed look she often used on her three small children, then continued. ''That leaves family and money. I know how crazy parents get about their kids. Think of that cheerleader mom, Wanda

What's-Her-Face. And you know that Hill man thinks you've been messing with his family, taking his girls away from him.''

''So how come he's not sending Amanda letters?'' I asked. ''He knew her name, and she was just as involved in taking the girls as I was. More so, because she had the contacts at Children's Protective Services.''

''Do you have to get so nitpicky? We're just brainstorming here.''

I cut her off. ''And another thing. I got the first letter before I even talked to the Hill kids.''

Margaret, as always, had an answer ready. ''But you wrote the story about him, didn't you? Maybe he was mad about that.''

Maybe. And John's sister-in-law had mentioned that he'd been in graduate school. A smart, violent man. At first I thought Hill wouldn't be the type to bother writing letters, but now I wasn't so sure.

''And as for money,'' Margaret continued, ''I've been thinking about that too. Obviously you didn't do anything purposely. You have a lot of annoying traits, Lizzy, but, let's face it, you don't have a malicious bone in your body.''

''Remind me to put it in my will that I don't want you to give my eulogy,'' I said sourly.

Margaret ignored me. ''So that leaves unintentional crimes, something you might not even have realized you did. The obvious things, of course, are job-related. Did you refuse to hire someone or maybe get someone fired?'' When I shook my head, she added, ''Give someone a lousy recommendation for a new job?''

''Right offhand I can't think of anything like that. I have

been a reference for several people, but not lately. And I was always very complimentary.''

I tried to think of workers I had complained about: a sloppy printing job on a center brochure that had to be reprinted, my complaint in the business office that I was always getting someone else's mail in my box. But I doubted that anyone had been fired because of my complaints. But what if they had? What if the employee I'd complained about was already in hot water with his supervisor and my criticism was the last straw?

''Or say you did something that you thought was helpful—maybe advised someone to take a new job—and he followed your advice and hated the job or got laid off right away. Maybe he blamed you: 'I'd be perfectly happy in my old job if I hadn't listened to that damn Liz James.' ''

Fortunately at this moment Margaret glanced at her kitchen clock. ''Oh, gee, I need to go pick up Maria at preschool. You want to come with me?''

''No, thanks. I need to get going myself.'' All this talk of crimes I might have committed was making me feel queasy again.

Margaret pulled a pair of sweatpants over her leotard. ''There's another possibility. Maybe you did nothing and some guy is just fixated on you for no good reason—say, you look like his ex-wife or his mean aunt who abused him when he was a kid.''

''Now that's a comforting thought.'' I was beginning to wish I'd stayed at work.

Margaret grabbed her purse and car keys. As we walked to our cars, she gripped my shoulder. ''You know, Liz, maybe you should take that policewoman's advice and get out of town until this blows over. I know Mom would love to have you come visit.''

I WENT back to work the next morning with something resembling relief. I'd more or less proved to myself that I couldn't sit at home doing nothing, waiting for my poison-pen writer to be exposed. With nothing to do, I'd spent the day obsessing about what I might have done—continuing Margaret's uplifting train of thought. The mental wheel-spinning drove me nuts. I needed to be mentally occupied. I also needed to be paid regularly. I couldn't afford to go on an indefinite, unpaid leave of absence.

So here I was back at the mental health center, feeling exhausted after a sleepless night of considering possible slights or unintended sins I might have committed. The stack of papers I needed to attend to looked like a lifeline. Here was something tangible I could focus on. I set to work editing Amanda's journal article on abused children with a determined ferociousness.

I was well into the article when I heard the commotion in the hallway. Several people were talking in agitated but muffled voices down the hall. I decided to ignore them.

I was tightening up a somewhat flowery paragraph when someone stepped into my office. I looked up, into the red-rimmed eyes of Missy Gould.

''Did you hear what happened?'' She shook her head in disbelief, then started to cry. ''I can't believe it!''

''Missy, what's wrong?''

Through her tear-filled eyes she tried to focus on me. ''It's Lauren. We just heard about her.''

Had Donna gone ahead and fired the girl? ''What about Lauren?''

"She's dead!" Missy burst into loud sobs.

I stared at her, feeling suddenly chilled to the bone. "How?" I demanded, my voice insistent and too loud.

"Car accident," Missy wailed. "She died last night on the way home from work."

Chapter Eighteen

I RODE TO LAUREN'S FUNERAL WITH DONNA HUBBARD. The service was in Clear Lake City, a newish, upper-middle-class kind of town that had grown up around the Johnson Space Center.

"I talked to her mother the day after the accident," Donna told me as she maneuvered her navy Pontiac onto the on-ramp for the Gulf Freeway. "The poor woman was just distraught." Donna shook her lacquered helmet of hair at the memory. "You know Lauren was driving to their house for dinner when she had the accident."

"Oh, how awful." I'd been wondering what Lauren had been doing on the freeway going to Galveston. Her apartment was in a huge complex near the Medical Center. "I'm sure if that happened to my child, I'd be telling myself, 'She'd be alive today if only I'd invited her to come another night.' "

Donna accelerated onto the freeway. "Unfortunately parents do tend to blame themselves for everything bad that happens to their child. Even when the child is grown up and making decisions totally at odds with everything her parents taught her."

I squinted at her. Clearly Donna knew something about the accident that I didn't. Knowing her penchant for secrecy and sanctimoniousness—Donna's twin S's—I guessed she wouldn't tell me, but I made a stab at it anyway. "Are you saying the accident was Lauren's fault?"

She didn't answer at first. But finally, sounding as if she was weighing each word, she said, "I'm suggesting that Lauren's judgment was impaired when she was driving."

"She was drunk?" I translated.

Donna shook her head. "From what I heard she'd been using drugs." She sighed. "Lauren seemed to be having quite a problem with that lately."

"Do you know what kind of drug she was on the night she died?"

"Some kind of hallucinogen. LSD, I think. A police officer told me they found it in her bloodstream when they did the autopsy."

"Oh, how awful!" I remembered Lauren's unfocused eyes, her mocking accusation, "You're such a do-gooder, Liz." Had that been only a week ago? Why had Lauren suddenly started taking drugs at work? From some of her coy stories about her "wild weekends," I'd always suspected that Lauren was a heavy social drinker and not immune to a bit of drug experimentation. But why had her drug use suddenly escalated?

"It's a tragedy when young people turn to drugs," Donna said.

Her moralistic tone irritated me. Although Donna was in fact only fourteen years older than I—not old enough to be my mother—she always made me feel irrationally defensive, as if I was somehow included in her blanket condemnation of "young people." I mentally cursed the two women from human resources who were supposed to have driven with us but bowed out at the last minute. Spending ninety minutes alone in a car with Donna Hubbard was not the kind of experience I relished.

"Speaking of young people," I said, wanting to change the subject, "how is Jennifer doing? Is she driving in for the funeral?" The summer she'd worked at the center, Donna's daughter had spent a lot of lunch hours with Lauren.

"Oh, Jennifer wanted to come, but she had a term paper that was due and a midterm to study for, so I told her to stay in Austin and do her work. I'd give the family her condolences."

That sounded like Donna. I was even mildly surprised that she was interrupting her workday to attend the funeral.

"Jennifer and Lauren were really not that close," Donna continued. "I know they were quite friendly that one summer, but it was one of those casual friendships based on being the same age and working in nearby offices. The two of them really had nothing in common. Once Jennifer went to college, they drifted apart."

I remembered the girls as being more than quite friendly that summer, but I could see how their friendship could have lapsed once Jennifer moved away. Lauren, as I recalled, was a possessive, jealous friend. Jennifer once told me Lauren had even complained that she was spending too much time with me: "It's like Lauren thinks my only friend should be her." I hoped Jennifer had found some less demanding friends in Austin.

We drove the rest of the way more or less in silence, not exactly unfriendly, more of a mutual recognition that we were two people who had absolutely nothing to say to each other. Donna, at least, had a terrific sense of direction. Within five minutes of exiting the freeway, she was pulling into the parking lot of the tan brick Methodist church. We joined the throng of somberly dressed middle-aged couples and a group of teenage girls hurrying to the church.

The sanctuary was one of those modernistic high-ceilinged places with abstract stained glass windows and a starkness I didn't like. It felt more impersonal than the smaller, more traditional church Nat had belonged to, but this was probably my own bias against institutional architecture of the fifties and sixties that seemed the equivalent of those awful big-finned sixties cars.

The service seemed in keeping with the building: glib and filled with overblown sentiments. The jowly, middle-aged minister, who looked as if he was wearing a toupee, spoke at length of the wrenching tragedy of losing this "young and vital woman before she'd hardly begun her life's journey." He described pigtailed little Lauren at her first ballet recital, the gap-toothed cherub singing in the church Christmas pageant.

I tried hard to squelch my suspicion that the man had never met Lauren, that he was just pulling out some generic girl memories. Certainly he was not describing the young woman I knew. Mentally I supplied my own adjectives for that Lauren: gossipy, possessive, immature. Immediately I felt like a grade-A shit. Why had I come to the funeral of someone I'd never honestly liked? "Because," Lauren's mocking voice sounded in my head, "you're a do-gooder and a hypocrite."

Finally the service was over. As we filed slowly out of the church I caught the eye of Missy Gould, who'd been sitting with two young women who worked in the business office. All three of the women looked as if they'd been crying.

"I'd like to speak to the family," Donna said, glancing

toward a corner of the vestibule where Lauren's parents stood surrounded by a cluster of people. We joined the line waiting to offer their condolences.

"I'm so sorry," I told Lauren's mother, who nodded at me, her face expressionless. She looked like an older version of her daughter. Lauren had inherited her mother's high cheekbones, dark hair, and large eyes. Lauren's face, though, had been more animated, always expressing some intense reaction to events—astonishment, despair, elation. But perhaps under other circumstances Mrs. Jones would have been animated too. I explained to the mother that I'd worked with Lauren at the mental health center.

"Thank you for coming," she said woodenly.

I moved on to Mr. Jones, who told me that Lauren had spoken a lot about her coworkers. "She had a lot of friends there," he said, then swallowed several times.

"Yes, she did." I moved on, giving Donna a turn to speak.

When I stepped to the side, I saw Donna was still talking to Mrs. Jones. But this time Lauren's mother was nodding her head in agreement, responding at length to whatever Donna had said.

When we were back in her car, Donna said, "The father won't admit that Lauren was taking drugs, but her mother knew. She couldn't do anything about it. Lauren wouldn't listen to her any more than she listened to me when I tried to counsel her."

I stared at her. Surely this wasn't what she and Mrs. Jones had been talking about minutes ago. But then I remembered Donna had mentioned speaking to Lauren's mother earlier on the phone.

Donna sighed as she drove out of the church parking lot.

"She put so much time and attention into that girl. When they're little you see all this potential in the child, you see everything they can grow up to be."

Donna's face suddenly looked sad, somehow older. "And then this happens," she said, shaking her head. "Her mother told herself that Lauren would outgrow this adolescent rebellion. But now Lauren never will."

Chapter Nineteen

I HADN'T SEEN NICK SINCE THE NIGHT I WALKED OUT on him. We hadn't even talked to each other on the phone in the intervening weeks. So Nick Finley was not the person I expected to see saunter into my office, looking for all the world as if everything was exactly the way it used to be between us.

''What do you want?'' I'd been back in my office only twenty minutes. The funeral and being trapped in a car with Donna had taken their toll.

Nick studied my black and white plaid dress. ''You go to Lauren's funeral?''

I nodded.

''How was it?''

I shrugged. ''About what you'd expect. Did you come here to ask me about the funeral?''

''No.'' Uninvited, he perched on a corner of my desk. ''I need to talk to you.'' He held up one finger to stop me from interrupting. ''I know you're pissed at me—we can talk about that later if you want—but we need to clear things up about Lauren.''

About Lauren? ''Why?'' Then it hit me. ''You mean for your story?''

''No.'' Nick ignored the surge of hostility emanating from my direction. ''Look,'' he said, leaning down so he could peer into my eyes, "Lauren was my number one suspect for the killer. And now she's dead."

My curiosity was stronger than my anger. "I thought you said before that Lauren wasn't smart enough to plan out the murders."

"I changed my mind. Lauren was street-smart and sneaky. She could have done it. The more I talked to her, the more I saw how volatile and unstable she was, really messed up on drugs. One day she was friendly and kind of hyper, talking a mile a minute about Nat, how she didn't think she could ever love anyone else. The next time I talked to her she was slurring her words together, suddenly furious with me, telling me I'd be sorry if I wrote what she'd told me—which, as far as I could see, wasn't much."

I nodded. "She turned on me too for no apparent reason. But that doesn't mean she killed anybody. In fact, considering how well planned the murders seemed to be, I'd be more likely to think Lauren's drug use was a perfect alibi—she wasn't functioning well enough to pull off the killings."

Nick shrugged. "Maybe. But from what I heard, it was only recently that Lauren's work performance began to slip—after Nat died."

"I guess that's true." Lauren's work had never been stellar, but certainly it had deteriorated noticeably in the last few weeks.

Nick stood up. "Come on. I want you to go with me to Lauren's apartment."

"What?" I stared at him. Had he lost his mind? "Why would we want to do that?"

"To look for—something. I don't know what. Evidence that Lauren killed Nat and Gina. Evidence that she didn't."

"Why would Lauren kill Gina? They barely knew each other."

He grabbed my hand and pulled me to my feet. "I'll tell you in the car."

I shook free from his grasp. "No, this is a really stupid idea, Nick. How are you planning to get into Lauren's apartment?"

He grinned. "I'll think of something. Come on, Liz, I want to get there before her relatives arrive to clean out the place. I need your help."

"Maybe they've already cleaned it out. Or maybe a roommate is there right now, sitting in the living room watching TV."

"Maybe. But we'll never know until we get there, will we?" Nick probably thought he was offering me an ingratiating smile. It looked more like a grimace.

"I don't want to do this, Nick. I've got tons of work to do, and I just got back from the girl's funeral, for God's sake. It seems so ghoulish to rifle through someone's apartment on the day she's buried."

Nick did not disagree. "But it might be our last chance. Maybe our only chance. The apartment is probably paid up until the end of the month, next Tuesday." He sent me a level gaze and played his trump card. "And I'm going there now. With or without you."

I went, telling myself that Nick desperately needed my assistance—my help in getting past the apartment manager, my insights into Lauren, my ability to quickly rummage through drawers. But the real reason I went was that I couldn't bear not knowing immediately what Nick discovered. If Lauren had killed Nat and Gina and sent all of us those awful letters, I'd sleep a lot better at night knowing that the danger was over.

As Nick drove to Lauren's apartment, I thought about what he'd told me. Lauren could have written the letters. It would have been easy for her to slip into my office to drop off a message; she was in and out of my office all the time. Certainly her do-gooder crack could be interpreted as evidence of her resentment of me. And she, the gossip queen of the mental health center, could easily have found out what nights Gina worked late and when Nat wouldn't have a client in his office. Anyone seeing Lauren in the hall outside their offices would have thought nothing of it. She regularly stopped in to chat with friends throughout the center.

There was only one major flaw in this theory. I turned to Nick. "So why would Lauren want to murder Gina?"

Nick's smile, I thought, was irritatingly smug. "Gina knew about Lauren's drug use. She told Lauren if she didn't stop using them either on her own or in a drug rehab program, she'd see that Lauren was fired."

"Who told you that?"

"Olivia Dickson."

It figured. "Olivia hates Lauren. She's been telling everyone who'll listen how insanely jealous Lauren was of Nat. An evaluation, of course, which has nothing to do with the fact that Nat dumped Olivia when he started dating Lauren."

"That still doesn't mean Olivia is lying. Presumably she was once very close to Gina. Even after their affair ended, they still worked together. Probably Gina told Olivia right after she'd confronted Lauren."

"Yeah, I guess that could have happened. Even Todd,

Gina's ex-husband, said how vehement Gina was about drugs—almost fanatical. I could see her trying to push Lauren into treatment.''

Nick pulled into the visitor's parking lot at the huge apartment complex where Lauren had lived. The place looked well-maintained, with the apartments grouped around four courtyards, each with a swimming pool in the middle. The manager's office was at the front of the first courtyard.

Nick saw where I was heading. ''Let's try her apartment first.'' He pulled a scrap of paper from his wallet. ''It's number 262.''

Lauren's apartment was on the second floor of the second cluster. As we approached the door I wondered what we were supposed to say if someone actually opened the door when we knocked.

This possibility apparently did not bother Nick. He knocked loudly on the door. ''Let me do the talking,'' he whispered.

''You bet.''

No one answered. Nick knocked again, waited sixty seconds, then tried the door handle. Unsurprisingly, it was locked.

''What now, Sherlock?''

He shook his head. ''Oh, ye of little faith.'' He turned toward the stairs. ''Now we try the manager's office.''

The manager, a gaunt, gray-haired woman, was in her office. From the smell of the place, she was probably a chain-smoker. Also not the friendliest person in the world.

I let Nick provide the explanation. He'd stopped back at his car to pick up some paper sacks and three cardboard boxes—his props. He was Lauren's brother, he explained.

We were here to clean up and move out some of her things.

From behind her metal desk, the old lady studied us, her eyes narrowed, lips pressed into a hard line. The expression of someone who even now was setting off a security alarm under her desk.

Finally she spoke. "I thought the girl's parents were coming to clear out the place. The mother called yesterday."

Nick nodded knowingly. "Oh, they're still coming to move Lauren's furniture and pack up her clothes. We just came to clean up the place—empty the refrigerator, toss out the stuff Mother and Daddy don't want to take." Nick paused for a moment, smiling sadly. "If you'd like some identification . . ."

Identification? I could feel my palms growing clammy. I tried hard to look trustworthy.

The flinty eyes darted from Nick to me. Were these the faces of thieves? I myself would have voted yes, but fortunately the manager was a less suspicious woman than I. "Now what apartment was she in again?" she asked.

"Two sixty-two," Nick answered.

Apparently reassured, the manager retrieved the proper key and led us back to Lauren's apartment. She unlocked Lauren's door for us. "When you leave lock the bottom lock from the inside and just pull the door shut."

"Sure thing," Nick said. "And thanks for your help."

I rolled my eyes at him once we were inside with the door closed. "You certainly have a nice little talent for lying."

"Thanks, ma'am, I try."

Lauren's apartment was a smallish one-bedroom decorated sparsely with what looked like furniture borrowed from her parents: a plaid upholstered couch with a matching chair, and an early American end table in the living room, a walnut table and chair that badly needed refinishing in the dining room. At least, I saw as I walked into the bedroom with its queen-sized bed, we didn't have to contend with a possible roommate walking in on us, though I would have been a lot more comfortable if the manager had mentioned when Lauren's parents were planning to come pack up her stuff.

"What a slob!" Nick said as he stepped around piles of Lauren's dirty clothes lying on the bedroom floor.

"Uh, just what exactly are we looking for?" I inquired.

He picked up an address book sitting on the nightstand. "When we find it, I'll let you know." He pointed to a chest of drawers. "Why don't you start looking through that?"

Reluctantly I set about my task. I opened the top drawer, which was filled with Lauren's very skimpy underwear, feeling like a voyeur. There was nothing but a jumble of bras and panties in the first drawer. I moved on to the second. It was filled with peekaboo nightgowns and a nice assortment of teddies. "Hey, look at this," I said, holding up a black garter belt.

Nick glanced over and whistled. "You might have found something. Maybe the garter belt around Nat's neck was a memento of some special evening the two of them shared. Did the garter belt you saw look like this one?"

I glared at him. "I didn't notice. Strangely enough, it didn't occur to me to really inspect it. All I remember is that it was black."

"Well, let's take this one with us. We don't want her parents throwing away possible evidence. Maybe you're on a roll, Liz. See if you can find anything else."

I didn't. In forty-five minutes of snooping the only other thing I discovered was that Lauren had had a lot of clothes. As each minute passed, I was growing more nervous. "Nick," I called into the walk-in closet, "I vote for taking the garter belt and getting the hell out of here."

He emerged from the closet holding two large-sized baggies, the kind with zip-locked tops.

I moved closer to inspect the contents. Inside one were three joints. The second bag was about a third full of a white powdery substance.

Nick opened the second bag and touched a finger to the powder. He sniffed his finger, then tasted it. "It's cocaine all right."

"Where did you find it?"

He pointed to the top shelf of the closet. "Up there. In a shoe box."

"Were there any other drugs there?"

Nick shook his head. "This was it. I even checked all the other shoe boxes on the floor, but all they contained was shoes."

"But Donna said the autopsy found some kind of hallucinogen in Laura's bloodstream."

Nick shrugged. "So maybe she took the last of it."

I glanced at the digital clock on Lauren's nightstand. Its large red numbers informed me that it was now 4:26. "We really need to get out of here, Nick. Neighbors will be coming home from work soon, and I don't want them asking me what we're doing here."

"Some of the neighbors I've had over the years wouldn't notice if a group of Hell's Angels drove their motorcycles out my front door," Nick grumbled. But I noticed he nevertheless seemed to pick up his pace. "We'll be out of here in fifteen minutes; I promise."

I didn't find anything else of interest until I started searching the kitchen. In the cabinet drawer closest to the wall phone I found a small legal pad covered with Lauren's swirly, little-girl handwriting and a small, imitation-leather diary.

Curious, I scanned the diary notations. Lauren was not the kind of person I expected to put her intimate thoughts on paper. Even when she took phone messages for me, she just wrote down a name and phone number, never any note about what the caller had said.

But apparently the diary stimulated her urge to write. Although many of the entries were only a few lines, Lauren seemed to have written a detailed account of her romance with Nat. Or at least her version of the relationship.

"It's like a romantic fairy tale," I said to Nick after I read a few pages detailing their "sewful kises." "Except Lauren is a terrible speller and she doesn't believe in commas or even periods. Hell, half of her sentences don't even have verbs." After reading the diary, it was hard to believe that Lauren had managed to graduate from high school.

Nick walked over and paged through the diary. We looked at each other.

I voiced what both of us were thinking. "Lauren could never have written me those letters. There wasn't a chance in the world she could have correctly spelled 'accountable.' "

Chapter Twenty

WE LEFT AT 5:03 ACCORDING TO LAUREN'S KITCHEN clock, taking the garter belt, her diary, and a few pages of her scribbled phone notes with us. The drugs, the baggies wiped clean, went back on the shelf in the closet.

I was afraid that someone was going to question us once we stepped outside, but no one was around. Nick and I were each carrying a bag of trash, in case we ran into the apartment manager. Nick had insisted we sort through the contents of Lauren's wastebaskets, but all we'd found were a lot of empty frozen dinners cartons and plastic Diet Coke bottles, handfuls of wadded Kleenex, and an empty container of birth control pills—nothing exciting like a syringe, a stash of heroin, or a pocket-sized billy club.

After seeing Lauren's diary, I wasn't even sure why we'd bothered to take the garter belt. It no longer seemed like evidence, only one item from Lauren's vast collection of sexy lingerie. ''What's the point in taking this stuff?'' I asked Nick as we dumped the trash in the metal bin at the edge of the parking lot. ''I think it's pretty clear that Lauren wasn't the killer.''

''What makes you think that?''

''You *saw* her diary.''

''So that means she didn't send the letters. She still could have killed Nat.''

"Nat got a note too. And Gina."

Nick sighed as he unlocked my car door. "So maybe several different people are involved. Maybe the letters had nothing to do with the deaths. We just assumed they were connected because the letters started shortly before Gina died. Who knows, maybe a lot of other people at the center—living, breathing people—received the letters too, and you just don't know about it."

It was a possibility that I'd also considered. Perhaps some disgruntled employee or dissatisfied patient had fired off letters to everyone who'd ever annoyed him: the guy who cut into line at the vending machine, the woman who hadn't returned his greeting in the hallway, or the therapist who kept him waiting half an hour and didn't even apologize. Or maybe the PR specialist who misquoted him in the center newsletter. Using this level of misdeed—the irritating rather than some grievous wrong—I was sure there were dozens of people I'd offended. I just wished I was totally convinced that the worst thing my anonymous correspondent intended to do to me was send me snotty letters.

I decided to change the subject. "I've been meaning to ask you, what would you have done if that apartment manager *had* wanted to see your ID?"

Nick flashed me his cocky grin. "I would have searched my pockets and said, 'Oh, gee, I must have left my wallet in my sports coat. I'll go get it; it's in my car.' " His smile expanded. "And then I would have gotten the hell out of there."

"Leaving *me* in the manager's office?"

He leaned over and patted my thigh. "I was hoping you'd have enough sense to say, 'Oh, that boy can't keep his head screwed on straight without my help,' and then hightail it right after me.''

Nick sent me a sidelong glance. ''I'm getting hungry. You interested in picking up some barbecue? We could take it to your place and read Lauren's diary together.''

I hesitated. I wasn't over being angry with Nick; I was still convinced that any long-term relationship between us was bound to fail. On the other hand, I *did* want to know what was in Lauren's diary.

Nick braked for a red light and turned innocent blue eyes on me. ''And I promise to behave this time.''

I laughed. ''That I've got to see. We need to go pick up my car, though. If you get the barbecue, I'll meet you back at my place.'' I looked at him. ''I'd like the chicken plate with sides of potato salad and coleslaw. And extra sauce.''

''What?'' he said. ''No links or ribs?''

I had the table set by the time Nick arrived with Luther's take-out bags. ''You want a beer?'' I called from the kitchen.

''That would be great.'' Nick had already pulled out the diary and was scanning it. ''Now, do you really think Nat told her he was consumed—spelled c-u-n-s-o-o-m-e-d—with desire for her day and night?''

I considered it. ''It does sound like Lauren lifted it from a romance novel, doesn't it?''

Nick took a bite of his sandwich and kept reading. ''Clearly this girl is deep into romantic fantasy. She sounds really out of touch with reality.''

I wasn't so sure. Couldn't Lauren have just written out her own idealized romance—the way she wished her relationship with Nat was—without really believing it was that way? How many girls over the years had scribbled their imagined married names in their school notebooks? Probably Lauren was doing essentially the same thing with her purple prose.

I washed down a mouthful of barbecued chicken with a swig of Coors Light. ''Check to see what she wrote about a month ago, a couple weeks before Nat died. That's when I overheard her and Nat arguing in her office.''

Nick flipped through the diary pages. Apparently finding what he wanted, he started reading. A few minutes later he looked up. ''Nothing. She never even mentions any argument with Nat, and I read all the way to the end.''

''She doesn't even suggest they're having any problems?''

Nick shook his head. ''She says they were getting married. In June, at her church in Clear Lake. Big wedding, lots of bridesmaids, the works.''

Was it possible that Lauren and Nat had resolved their differences? Perhaps their argument had turned out to be trivial, a lovers' spat. Now that I thought about it, neither Lauren nor Nat had ever told me they'd broken up. I tried to remember who had told me that. Olivia! Hardly a disinterested party. But was she a liar?

''And get this,'' Nick said, moving his finger down a page of the diary. ''The weekend before Nat died, Lauren bought her wedding dress.''

''Oh, how awful.'' No wonder Lauren had acted like the bereaved widow at Nat's funeral. ''What did she write about Nat's death?''

Nick looked up at me. ''Nothing.''

''*Nothing?*''

''Buying her wedding dress was the last entry.''

• • •

THE FULL impact of Lauren's death didn't really hit me until the next morning. When I walked into her office to fill my coffee mug, someone new was sitting at Lauren's desk. "Hi," she said, looking up from her work, a gaunt, middle-aged woman with graying brown hair. "I'm Nelda Jordan, a temp."

I smiled, introduced myself, poured my coffee, and got out fast. Somehow having someone else in Lauren's chair was more unsettling than her empty desk had been.

In the hallway I almost collided with Donna Hubbard. "Oh, Donna, I'm sorry. Did I spill any coffee on you?" I inspected her immaculate gray suit for a stain.

"No damage done." Donna glanced into Lauren's office. She lowered her voice. "It seems eerie in there without her, doesn't it?"

That was it exactly: eerie. "I guess I just walked in, not thinking, expecting to see her."

Donna nodded, turned toward her office.

"You know I always meant to ask you about Lauren's last day," I said. "I went home sick that day, but I didn't remember Lauren acting particularly unusual that morning. Maybe a little subdued." When Donna didn't leap in to add her two cents to the conversation, I added, "Did *you* think she seemed different that day?"

Donna's expression made it clear that she wasn't thrilled about wasting time chatting in the hallway. "She wasn't using drugs on the job if that's what you mean."

It wasn't actually, but I sensed that my allotted ninety seconds of Donna's workday were rapidly dwindling. "Do you know what time she left work that day?"

"Yes, about 5:15." The look of impatience left Donna's face, replaced with something resembling sadness. "I asked her to stay late to discuss her work performance. She assured me she was no longer using drugs, and I had no reason not to believe her. I said I was glad she had worked out her problems. Then she left. She told me she was going to her parents' house for dinner that night. Her father was grilling steaks.''

If it had been anyone other than Donna standing in front of me, I probably would have leaned over and patted her shoulder. I doubted that Donna, though, would have appreciated the gesture. ''It seems so strange that she would have taken LSD right before she had to make a long drive to her parents' house.''

Donna nodded. ''Yes, it was very strange.'' This time she continued to her office. ''But who can tell about kids these days?'' she said as she passed me.

By the time I got back to my office my coffee was lukewarm. I drank it anyway, reluctant to return to Lauren's office.

I was scanning my mail when I sensed someone was standing in my doorway. I glanced up.

''Hi.'' It was Olivia Dickson.

''Hi, Olivia.'' I wondered how long she'd been standing there watching me. And why.

She glided into my office, looking tall and sleek in an emerald tunic and black slacks. She didn't bother to sit down, just stood next to my desk, peering down at me. ''Did you know I quit my job?''

''No, I didn't. When are you leaving?''

''End of the week.''

She hadn't given much notice. ''What are you going to do?''

She shrugged, making the gesture look insouciant. ''Who

knows? All I'm sure of at this point is that I want out. I'm telling myself I'm taking a sabbatical.''

A convenient way to view unemployment. ''Well, good luck,'' I said, not sure what else to say. I was surprised that Olivia had even bothered to tell me she was leaving.

''Thanks. I was hoping we could have lunch before I left. Can you do it today or tomorrow?''

I didn't really want to have lunch with her. We'd barely spoken to each other in the years she'd worked here. Why start now, on her last week of work?

Sensing my hesitation, Olivia added, ''There's something I need to tell you before I go. Something vitally important to your welfare.''

Chapter Twenty-one

"I'M SICK OF WAITING IN LINE AT ALL THOSE HOSPITAL cafeterias," Olivia said as she drove us in her green MG down Holcombe Boulevard. "I want a place with waiters and real tablecloths for a change."

She suggested we eat at Luigi's, a little Italian place near the medical center, which was fine with me. Or at least it would have been if I were eating there with someone else. I still wasn't thrilled at the prospect of spending an hour alone with Olivia, and I hadn't yet heard any piece of news remotely important to my well-being.

At the restaurant Olivia insisted that we be seated at a corner table, as far away as possible from the other diners. When the waiter came she ordered spaghetti carbonara and a glass of Chianti, and I ordered pasta salad and iced tea.

"Sure you don't want some wine?" Olivia asked. "You look as if you could use a drink."

It came out, like most of Olivia's suggestions, sounding like a dig. "Actually, I'd love a glass, but whenever I drink at lunch, I feel like I need a nap at two-thirty." I waited until the waiter had departed. "Now, what was it you needed to tell me?"

Olivia, however, was not about to be rushed. She sipped at her wine and then spread a thick layer of butter on a piece of hot, crusty bread. How could she eat like this and still be so skinny? A little marathon running on the weekends? A full-blown case of bulimia?

Finally, though, she stopped chewing and sipping and directed her attention to my question. "First I want to ask you a few questions about the article Nick is writing."

It figured. I tore off a piece of bread and popped it into my mouth. I knew I should have come up with an excuse for why I couldn't go to lunch with her. "You'll have to ask Nick about that. He hasn't told me what he's going to write."

In fact the only way Nick and I had managed to remain civil with each other was by our tacit agreement not to discuss his story. At this point our truce was too shaky to even tiptoe around the topic.

"Oh, shit," Olivia said. "I was afraid of that."

"Just what is it you don't want Nick to print?" I inquired, not sure I even wanted to know.

Olivia took a swig of wine before answering. "I don't want him printing all the negative things I said about Lauren. About me suspecting that Lauren killed Nat."

"Now you don't think she did it?" Okay, so I did want to know what she'd told Nick.

Olivia delicately blotted her napkin against her thin lips. "I'm not so sure anymore. Lauren *was* unstable enough to kill Nat—and Gina too. And her drug use would have further distorted her judgment. I just didn't particularly want to see that opinion in print. It would sound like I was attacking some poor dead girl who couldn't defend herself." She raised her eyebrows at me. "As a matter of fact, I would prefer not to be quoted at all."

Wouldn't we all? I backtracked to the part that interested me. "Why do you think Lauren would kill Gina?" Nick had mentioned this, but I wanted to hear it from Olivia herself.

''Because Gina saw Lauren smoking dope one day and threatened to get her fired.''

''That doesn't seem like a reason to kill her. I never thought Lauren was particularly attached to that job. I could see her just laughing in Gina's face and telling her to fuck off.''

''That's exactly what she did tell her,'' Olivia admitted. ''Not that that would have made Gina back off.'' She seemed to hesitate, then added, ''There was more to it than that, of course.''

''Oh?''

''Well, Gina was *insane* about drugs. Her dad was an alcoholic, and her younger sister died because she was on drugs. She was walking down the middle of a freeway at night, high on something, and a truck hit her.''

Olivia sighed. ''That was one of the reasons I thought at first that Gina had committed suicide—you know, she and her sister both dying from drugs. I thought Gina might have still felt guilty about not helping her sister.''

Oh, spare me! I wanted to snap at her. Did therapists never stop spouting these convoluted theories—which anyone with any common sense at all would know were not true? Still I guessed it was possible that there might be some connection between Gina's death and her sister's. Could someone have blamed Gina for that death? And how many people at the mental health center besides Olivia knew how Gina's sister had died?

Olivia was still talking. ''. . . because Lauren had just started going out with Nat at that point,'' she said, looking embarrassed.

I realized I didn't have a clue what she was talking about. I decided to bluff. I tilted my head and wrinkled my brows in what I hoped was a puzzled expression. "And Lauren thought . . ."

"That Gina was having an affair with Nat."

"Why would she think that?" I wasn't faking the puzzled expression now.

"Because she overheard me tell Todd that when he cornered me in the cafeteria. Somebody had told him I worked with Gina." It was clear from the impatience in Olivia's voice that she'd already mentioned this part.

"But Gina didn't—"

"No." Olivia glared at me. "I just told Todd that because he kept pressing me about who Gina was having an affair with. Apparently she'd told him she'd been involved with someone, and he was obviously jealous."

Olivia sighed. "I know I shouldn't have given him Nat's name, but he'd just broken up with me, and I was hurt and angry. With him and with Gina. Gina told me what a short fuse Todd had, and I sure as hell wasn't about to admit to Mr. Macho that I was the person who'd been having sex with his ex-wife. If he was going to punch out Gina's ex-lover, let him hit Nat."

I thought back to the day I'd encountered Todd in the hall. "Do you remember when this was?"

Olivia's large eyes swiveled to the right as she thought about it. "It was two days before Gina died. I remember thinking about that at the memorial service."

"And you're sure Lauren overheard you talking to Todd?" As a rule Olivia spoke quickly and quietly; she did not have the kind of voice that would carry in a noisy cafeteria.

Olivia nodded. "It was after lunch and the place was almost empty. I didn't know Lauren was behind us. We were standing by the Coke machine with our backs to her. She was such an incredible gossip she was probably sneaking up on us to hear what we were talking about. But when I mentioned Nat's name I heard her gasp. I turned around and saw Lauren rushing toward the door."

I stared at her. So Lauren *did* have a motive for killing Gina, even if that reason was pure fabrication. I'd never thought that Gina threatening to get Lauren fired from her boring, low-paid job would have bothered Lauren much. But if she thought Gina might take Nat away from her . . . I had seen how irrationally jealous Lauren could be. Even my amused comments about the girls on my tour drooling over Nat had upset her.

If Lauren had viewed Gina—a beautiful, intelligent woman in the same profession as Nat—as a real rival, might not Lauren have decided to get rid of the competition? And, though I'd never noticed that Lauren had a particularly well-developed sense of irony, wouldn't a drug overdose be a fitting end for someone who was harassing Lauren about her use of recreational drugs?

And what about Todd? Hadn't Olivia also given him a motive to get rid of Nat, his ex-wife's supposed lover? I had seen for myself just how volatile Todd was. He had always been my choice for prime suspect in Gina's death. It was only when Nat too was murdered—a person I presumed Todd hadn't known—that I eliminated him from my suspect list. The killer, I'd reasoned, had to have a grudge against both Gina and Nat. Thanks to Olivia's lies, Todd probably did.

I jumped when a voice behind me inquired if I'd like

dessert. I was so lost in my thoughts that I hadn't seen the waiter hovering.

Olivia waited until the man returned with our coffee then said, "Listen, Liz, I don't know exactly how to tell you this. Especially since I've always thought of you as being a very rational kind of person."

She stopped and pulled at a long strand of blond hair. She began again. "I'm basically intuitive, so I don't have a lot of facts I can use to convince you."

I wanted to reach over and shake her, yell, Blurt it out! Instead I bit my lip and waited.

"I have this strong feeling," she said, "that I'm in great danger."

"From whom?"

She shook her head. "I don't know. I just have this strong sense of an evil presence at the center."

I didn't know what to say. "Why would this . . . presence harm you?" I finally managed to ask.

"I don't know." Her eyes welled with tears. "But I do know that something terrible is going to happen there. And I'm getting out while I still have a chance."

Olivia reached out to touch an icy hand to my arm. "And I wanted to warn you. You too are in danger, Liz. Very serious danger."

Chapter Twenty-two

IT WAS THE SECOND TIME IN THE LAST TWO WEEKS THAT someone had suggested I hightail it out of town. If Olivia alone had issued her melodramatic forebodings, I probably would have dismissed her warning as psychic hooey. But the combination of matter-of-fact Detective Ramirez and emotional Olivia rendering the same verdict made me want to sprint for my car. Two very different women were telling me, ''Danger ahead! Leave the area at once!''

The only problem was I had to finish my newsletter stories first. If the deadline for my copy wasn't the next day I would have been strongly tempted to immediately begin an indefinite leave of absence. I'd return to work when the killer was in jail. If I lived frugally, my savings could hold out for several months, and Nick had already offered his family's hill country cabin as a rent-free retreat. Hadn't I always said I wanted to write a novel? Here was the perfect opportunity in a serene, rustic location with no interruptions—and a very low crime rate.

Tomorrow I'd seriously consider it. For today I closed my office door, took a deep breath, and began my monthly race to my deadline. Whatever evil force might be lurking around the center could wait until next week to come looking for me.

It wasn't until several hours later, when I stood up to

stretch, that the thought occurred to me: What if Olivia was the killer and her little lunchtime warning was just another verbal poison-pen letter? What better way to scare me than to mention her premonition that evil forces were stalking me? And perhaps Olivia was leaving her job because she was afraid the police were closing in on her.

Despite all the evidence of Lauren's jealousy and drug use, I still found it hard to believe she was the killer. If Lauren had wanted to kill Nat, she probably would have marched into his apartment and shot him, not slipped into his office, banged him on the head, tied a garter belt around his neck, and sneaked out. It was too complicated, just not Lauren's style.

But was it Olivia's style? Maybe. Bright, complex, high-strung Olivia every day had had to face two lovers who had spurned her. Her colleagues, just down the hall from her, so she could easily ascertain when they were alone in their offices and no one else was in sight. Could she be quitting her job because she could no longer face viewing the scene of her crimes?

Nat, after all, had believed that Olivia had sent him the threatening note. He'd believed she was vengeful and duplicitous. Nat had been an insightful guy, and somebody who knew Olivia a lot better than I did. What if he was right? And if Olivia was the killer, did that mean she was still after me? And if so, why?

I did a few minutes of stretches, then decided I needed to get back to work. The question of Olivia would have to wait until I was through writing.

By the time I emerged from my office everyone else on my hallway seemed to have gone home. I glanced at my watch: 6:45. Surely there were other people in the building,

I reassured myself: janitors, therapists who had groups at night, colleagues who were working late. But as I walked to the rest room, the silent hallway and the line of closed doors made me uneasy, as if someone was lurking in the darkness watching me.

On the way back I decided to pick up a snack from the cafeteria. Something energizing and nutritious, like a Baby Ruth and a cup of vending-machine coffee.

No one was in the cafeteria either. Too bad. I'd hoped to see a security guard sitting at one of the tables, taking a coffee break.

I shouldn't let Olivia and her melodramatic warnings get to me, I told myself, as I grabbed my candy bar and cardboard coffee cup and hurried back to the safety of my office.

I heard the noise too late. From the corner of my eye I caught a movement by the stairwell and swiveled to see who was there. A big hand grabbed my shoulder.

He spun me around, splashing hot coffee on my hand. John Hill. Grinning down at me in a way that made my stomach lurch.

"We meet again." He laughed. "And this time there's just you and me. The Incredible Hulk isn't available for rescues anymore."

He planned to kill me too! The jowly, bearded face contorted, the little pig eyes radiating sadistic glee.

I threw the coffee, what was left of it, at his face. Then I turned and ran down the hallway, screaming at the top of my lungs.

He tackled me. I crashed to the ground, all the air knocked out of me.

I felt a hand grab my shoulder and flip me onto my back.

Then he straddled me, his huge weight on my rib cage, one hand holding down my flailing arms.

I tried to scream, but nothing came out. Not even after the huge fist slammed into my face. "That's for poking your nose into my business."

The fist came down again and again. The pain was unbelievable. I could hear the terrified whimpering in my ears, the smacking sound of his fist shattering bone. Taste the blood in my mouth.

"Hold it!" The deep voice came from behind Hill. "Or I'm going to shoot your damn head off!"

Was I imagining it? Through the blood and tears filling my eyes, I saw Hill's head jerk around, heard him grunt. I felt the pressure on my rib cage stop, glimpsed a man in a uniform. Then I passed out.

Chapter Twenty-three

"SO HOW ARE YOU FEELING TODAY?" HER ARMS FILLED with bags of Chinese take-out food, Amanda leaned over and kissed me gingerly on the top of my head.

It was one of the few places on my body that didn't hurt. "I look worse than I feel." Which was saying a lot. Hobbling out of bed that morning, I'd caught a glimpse of myself in the bathroom mirror. Not a pretty sight. My face was a palette of darkening bruises, my right eye almost swollen shut and my nose broken. I also had a couple of cracked ribs. And felt pretty awful too.

"Everyone at the center sends you their love," Amanda said as she started unpacking the food. "They're very concerned about you. Even Donna Hubbard told me to tell you to stay home as long as you need to recuperate."

The effect of the pain pill I'd taken earlier was starting to wear off. "I'm not sure yet when I'm coming back, but I'm only planning on staying home for a few more days."

Amanda was dumping hot and sour soup into two bowls and had her back to me. "I thought you were considering not coming back for a while, taking a leave of absence."

"I'm thinking about it." In fact I had more or less made up my mind to go on leave before John Hill had attacked me. Now both Nick and Margaret, my two self-appointed bodyguards, were pressuring me to leave immediately, move this weekend. Nick had made all the arrangements with his aunt for me to stay in her vacant cabin in the hill country and had promised to spend a week there with me, helping me get settled. Every day when Margaret came to visit she brought me some new essential item I needed to take with me to the cabin. And I was thinking more and more that maybe I should stay at work after all.

We sat down to lunch: the soup, fried rice, and some stir-fried vegetable dish that looked as if it had chunks of tofu in it. I picked at the food and watched Amanda eat her soup.

"What's your problem?" I asked. Her eyes seemed to be focusing on everything in my kitchen except me, which was not at all like her.

She flushed, then smiled ruefully. At least she didn't say, What problem? "I feel guilty about you," she said.

"Why?"

"Because I wasn't there. Because John Hill was looking for me too. Because I was the person who talked you into going to his house."

"Oh, spare me." Suddenly my head felt as if someone were hammering on it. "I hate it when women do that: make something they had nothing to do with their fault. You're holding yourself accountable for his crimes—and I bet John Hill doesn't feel guilty at all."

Amanda sighed. "I know. But I still wish I'd been there. If there'd been two of us . . ."

"Maybe next time," I snapped. "Maybe next time you will be."

I apologized a few minutes later when Amanda loaded the dishwasher. "I'm just so angry all the time. I seem to lash out at everyone."

"You have reason to be angry."

It was one of those soothing-shrink things she said sometimes that tended to annoy me. Today I let it pass. "First of all I'm pissed at John Hill. You know he'll probably be out of jail any minute? The police told Nick they could only hold him forty-eight hours. I'm furious that he assaulted me, that he blamed me for something I never did. And I'm furious with myself, that I couldn't protect myself or at least hurt him too."

"Your screaming brought the security guard. And you threw hot coffee in his face. That was fighting back."

"Right. I'm sure Hill is thinking, 'That's one scary broad. I'm not going to mess with *her* again.' "

Amanda smiled, told me she had to get back to work but she'd come again tomorrow.

I walked her to the doorway, glad to be alone. Maybe it was just the pain getting to me, but for probably the first time in my life I was impatient with talk. I didn't want to discuss feelings anymore, mine or anyone else's. Had any of the in-depth discussions of John Hill's anger, any of the therapy sessions—his or Jean's—changed his behavior one iota? I didn't think so. Instead all of us talkers, the humanist coterie, had been beaten down by sheer brute force. Two of us had been killed by it.

I phoned my sister and left a message on her machine not to come over this afternoon. I wanted to take a nap. I took another pain pill, then lay down on the couch. But I was too edgy to sleep. I tried to read one of the stack of magazines Margaret had brought, but my swollen eye made reading difficult and I had trouble focusing my attention.

The knock on my door startled me. Shit, Margaret must not have gotten my message.

I peered through the peephole. The bland, schoolboy-handsome face on the opposite side looked ready to sell me a BMW.

"What do you want?" I yelled through the door at Todd Murdock, a.k.a. Stan Baker.

"I want to talk to you," he yelled back.

No kidding. "What about?"

The handsome face contorted in irritation. "Will you just open the damn door?"

I was in no mood to be pushed around by another macho bully. "Go away or I'll call the police."

I waited to see if he'd leave. He didn't.

"Listen, Liz." The tone ingratiating now, slipping into salesman mode. "I only need five minutes of your time, tops. I just found out something I think is important. About Gina's death."

I opened the door with the chain on. "What?"

He sighed. "Can I come in or not?"

It flashed through my mind that this was not the smartest move in the world. Oh, sure, Officer, I invited the mass murderer into my place, but I never thought he'd turn on *me*. I managed to push the thought away. After all, John Hill was the killer, wasn't he?

"God, what happened to your face?" he asked as he got a better look at my face.

"An asshole beat me up." You know the type. I didn't let him ask any more questions. "So what did you find out?"

He followed me to the living room, sat down across from me on an upholstered chair. "Well, a couple days ago I was going through all the stuff I'd moved from Gina's place. I told the landlady to give her furniture and clothes to the Salvation Army, but I emptied all her desk drawers and files into some boxes and shipped them to California. The police had already looked through them, and hadn't found anything, but I thought they might have overlooked something. Something subtle that I might see."

"You found something?" I interrupted. My head hurt too much to wait for the end of the story.

"Yes." He reached into the inside pocket of his navy blazer and pulled out a folded piece of lined yellow legal paper. He handed it to me. "Read it."

I opened the paper, read the scrawled handwriting. The message was short. "Gina, You evil, self-righteous bitch. Do you really think you HELP people? No way. You RUINED my life. My life will be over by the time you read this. Don't deceive yourself, bitch. Don't rationalize your behavior, to quote the great Gina Lawrence. My death is Your Fault. I'd probably be alive today if I hadn't met you." The letter was signed J. H.

My stomach lurched, and not just from the pain pill. I reread the letter. No date, just Monday written at the top. "Do you know who J. H. is?"

"No, I hoped you might. I tried to contact that other friend of Gina's, Olivia Dickson, but they told me at the mental health center that she'd resigned. They said you were home sick."

A really chatty bunch, my colleagues. "It sounds like the letter is from one of her patients." The rounded, rather flowery handwriting looked to me like a woman's, but I might have been wrong about that.

I tried to think of the J. H.'s I knew. Of course! Jean Hill. She had been a patient of Gina's, and her sister had even said how much Jean disliked Gina. And it would be just like Jean to blame Gina for pushing her to leave John. Could Jean have sensed that John was about to kill her? Or maybe she couldn't bear her life any longer and was about to kill herself. From what I'd heard no one had seen or heard from Jean in two months.

"I thought it sounded like it came from a patient too," Todd was saying. "That's why I wanted to talk to Olivia because she and Gina worked together. I figured she might know who it was. Or know of any patient who'd died recently."

"Maybe you could phone Olivia," I said, wanting to get rid of him.

Todd shook his head. "No, I was at her apartment and talked to the manager. She said Olivia moved out yesterday."

Moved out already? The last I'd heard Olivia planned on working until the end of this week. What had made her change her mind? "Where did she move to?"

Todd shrugged. "The manager didn't know. Said she hadn't left any forwarding address. Hadn't even bothered to get her deposit back."

Why? I wondered. What was so urgent? I picked up the yellow paper. "You didn't happen to find an envelope with this, did you?" A postmark with the date and city where the letter was mailed might give us valuable information about the writer's identity. Though it seemed too much to hope for, perhaps J. H. had even included an return address.

"No envelope. I looked. The letter must have been in a desk drawer with her address book and stationery. Not in her files—the stuff the police were interested in."

"Did you find any other letters? Gina told me she'd received a threatening letter, but I had the impression it wasn't signed.'' I tried to remember exactly what Gina had told me the night she stayed at my apartment. Her threatening letter must have been anonymous; Gina told me she thought Todd had sent it. Did that mean that J. H. was out of the picture by then? Did Gina know that J. H. was dead?

Todd retrieved the yellow letter, read it again before folding it carefully. ''This is the only threatening letter I saw. From what Olivia said before, she or the police didn't find any other ones.''

''Maybe you should show this to the police.''

''Maybe.'' Todd put it back in his inside coat pocket, then studied me with narrowed eyes. ''You *sure* you don't know who this J. H. is?''

I hesitated, debating with myself whether or not to tell him my suspicions. Then the ridiculousness of my scruples hit me. Who was I trying to protect—John Hill? Jean Hill had not been heard of for months; even if she were still alive, it wasn't very likely that she'd come out of hiding to stalk Gina and Nat. The most believable scenario was that Jean sent the first letter, somehow John read it, and then began his own acts of vengeance. I told Todd about my suspicions, emphasizing that I had absolutely no proof to back them up.

Todd listened intently, his expression grim. ''You know where I can get in contact with this John Hill?'' he said at the end of my story.

''The last I heard he was in jail, but he's probably out on bond by now.''

''Any idea where he lives?''

I glanced away. What if J. H. was somebody Gina knew years ago, one of her patients from the state hospital or that private psychiatric hospital she'd worked in? "No, sorry, I don't."

Todd stood up. He handed me a business card with a Houston number scrawled on the bottom. "If you think of anything else, I want you to call me. I'm staying at the downtown Hyatt. I have a hunch that this letter is somehow connected to Gina's death, and I want to find out who sent it."

I walked him to the door. "Oh, Todd, I meant to ask you before. When you were questioning people about Gina, did you happen to talk to Nat Ryan?"

"Who?"

I repeated the name, carefully watching his face. Either he was a good actor or he didn't have a clue who I was talking about. "A psychologist in the adult clinic."

Todd narrowed his eyes. "Is he the other guy who died?"

"Yeah. I thought you might have heard some rumors that were going around about him."

He shrugged, looking indifferent. "Gina never mentioned him."

"No, I think they barely knew each other."

Todd gave me a look that said so why the hell did you ask me about him, then remembered he wanted my help and thanked me for seeing him. I locked the door behind him, feeling, if possible, even more confused.

I spent the rest of the afternoon trying to make sense of what I knew. Had Jean in fact written that letter to Gina? There was something vaguely familiar about that handwriting, as if I'd either seen it before or knew somebody whose writing looked similar. A woman.

But if Jean had written the letter and then either ran away

or was killed, did that mean John had decided to continue sending his own threatening letters to center employees? While I had absolutely no problem imagining John as Gina and Nat's killer—he had the violent, vengeful temperament, a motive of sorts, and, according to his sister-in-law, the brains to plan out the whole thing—I had a hard time envisioning him as the poison-pen writer. I could see Jean enjoying writing hateful notes, but not John. He was more of a lash out and hit somebody kind of guy.

So what did this mean? John had done the killing but someone else—maybe someone totally unrelated to him—had written the letters?

And what about Olivia? Had she too started receiving threats and decided to get out of town while she still had a chance? Olivia, after all, had been the cotherapist of Jean's group at the women's shelter. I'd quoted Olivia (though not much, since Gina was so much more quotable) in my story about the women's shelter. It wouldn't be at all surprising if John Hill decided that Olivia too was to blame for Jean's decision to leave him.

Unless, of course, J. H. was someone I'd never known. And Gina's and Nat's deaths were totally unconnected to either John or Jean Hill.

Frustrated, I grabbed a sheet of the notebook paper I keep by the phone and started a list: Suspects.

1. John Hill. He had motive, means, and opportunity. He was spotted near Nat's office on the afternoon of his death. Although the poison-pen letter part was iffy, John could have done that too. Jean had told me how paranoid John was, how sensitive to imagined slights. Conceivably John could have written the first letter to me after reading my battered women story, which described him (though didn't

mention his real name) in an unflattering light.

2. Todd. Yes, he was furious with Gina the night before she died and yes, maybe he could have been jealous of Nat if he believed Nat was Gina's lover. The only problem was I believed him today when he didn't recognize Nat's name. His look of monumental indifference—why should I give two hoots about this guy?—was too convincing to be faked.

3. Olivia. She had a grudge against both Gina and Nat. She was smart and had easy access to Gina's and Nat's offices. I still couldn't figure out what Olivia had against me—if indeed she also wrote the letters—but maybe she had imagined I was closer than I actually was to Gina. Or maybe she was just pissed that I barely mentioned her in my women's shelter story. And Olivia *could* have quit her job so suddenly because she was scared the police were closing in on her.

4. Lauren. She had a motive of sorts and was always flitting in and out of center offices, gossiping with her friends. But after reading her diary, I was convinced she didn't write the poison-pen letters. And I still thought the way Nat was murdered was not Lauren's style. Now, if someone had found Nat naked and shot to death in his own bed with a black garter belt lying nearby, then I might very well have suspected Lauren.

5. Jean Hill. Okay, she hated Gina and could easily have blamed Nat too for not putting her marriage back together again. She was smart too. But I couldn't see how Jean could have disappeared off the face of the earth and still managed to dart in and out of offices without anyone spotting her.

6. Emilio Garcia. He found Gina's body and he was nearby on the night Nat was killed. He could have slipped into their offices and killed both of them without anyone

noticing anything. Still that left the very big question of motive. Sure, Emilio was angry with Gina for accusing him of stealing, but was that a reason to kill her? And I didn't know what his motive would be for killing Nat.

I reread my list, then crossed off Todd, Lauren, and Jean. I put a question mark next to Emilio's name. That left John Hill and Olivia. Or someone whose motive eluded me. Suspect X. Someone bright, well-organized, and informed who had a grudge against Gina, Nat, and, yes, probably me. Someone who knew a lot about all three of us, someone who probably worked at the mental health center or was a patient. Someone whose hatred linked the three of us in a way I hadn't foreseen.

I stared at my writing, feeling the same way I did when I sat down with my nieces and nephew, trying to see the hidden picture in one of those colorful, three-dimensional drawings. I'd hold the book to my nose, move it back an inch at a time, the way the kids instructed me. "Can't you see it, Aunt Liz? The big elephant. It's there. Can't you see it?"

"I believe you, honey," I'd say. But, damn it, I couldn't see it.

Just the way I couldn't see the pattern to these deaths. And I knew it was there, just waiting to be uncovered.

Chapter Twenty-four

I PHONED DETECTIVE RAMIREZ THE NEXT MORNING, ostensibly to tell her about the letter Todd had found, but also to see if the police had made any progress in their investigations of Gina's and Nat's murders. I was, of course, also highly interested in the topic of where John Hill was currently spending his nights. As usual, the detective was not in, but I left a message for her to call me.

She phoned me back around 3:15, sounding tired. She'd been out all night on a homicide investigation, she said, and had only now come back to the station.

I explained about Todd's letter, feeling unreasonably annoyed with her. Yes, I was aware that the chances of the police solving a homicide dropped dramatically after the first forty-eight hours, and yes, the Houston Police Department had hundreds of other violent crimes to investigate besides the ones at the mental health center. But that still didn't make me feel any less dismissed, as if the police had given each death its forty-eight hours, had failed at discovering the murderer, and now had moved on to the next case. Our allotted time of police attention was up. Until the next murder.

"Yes, I know about that," the detective said. "Mr. Murdock came down here to talk to me yesterday afternoon."

"He did?" Todd must have gone to see her immediately

after he left my apartment. I tried to marshal my thoughts. "Was the letter helpful?"

Investigator Ramirez sighed. "Mr. Murdock seemed to think that Jean Hill had written the letter, but there's no proof of that. We don't even know when the letter was mailed or where it was sent from."

So did she expect Todd to bring in a notarized document from Jean's mother stating yes, no question about it, this was undeniably her daughter's handwriting? Then it hit me. I had a sample of Jean's handwriting in my files at work. "Jean Hill sent me a letter after I wrote a story about her." A whiny letter complaining that I'd misrepresented what she'd told me, but that was besides the point. "I'm sure I put it in my correspondence file."

I expected the detective to be excited by the news, or at least pleased. She wasn't. "It would be helpful if we could prove that it was Mrs. Hill's handwriting, but, as I explained to Mr. Murdock, that isn't enough concrete evidence to link Ms. Lawrence's death to John Hill."

"How about interrogating Hill? His wife is missing, you know. And he *did* assault me."

"He *was* questioned. He didn't admit to anything. Said his wife left him, and he doesn't know where she is."

And what about his attack on me? Surely he couldn't deny that when there were two witnesses—me and the security guard—who could testify against him.

As if she sensed what I was going to say, Investigator Ramirez added, "He might be convicted of the assault charge, but, frankly, I don't see him serving much time. Not for a first offense."

The prospect of John Hill being free to stalk me again was not something I wanted to think about. "Hill was seen in the hallway outside Nat's office on the afternoon he died,'' I reminded the detective. What did the HPD need before they pressed charges—a Polaroid shot of the perpetrator committing the crime?

''We're working on it, Liz.'' This time I could hear the impatience underlying the politeness. ''Listen, I need to get back to this crime scene. Just two things. If you see Mr. Murdock again I suggest you strongly discourage him from going after John Hill himself. Although he seemed to doubt it, the police are still very involved in this case. Secondly, I want to let you know that John Hill should be out on bond today.''

My entire body started shaking. ''You—you think he might come after me again?''

''Probably he won't. He's already in enough trouble with the police. But I just want you to be on the alert.''

She did not sound convincing. Both she and I knew that the only person who could accurately predict John Hill's future behavior was about to get out of jail—if he wasn't out already. And so far that man had not been noted for either his caution or his impulse control.

''Liz?''

I took a deep breath, tried hard to focus. ''Yes?''

''I know I said it before, but I'd like you to seriously consider going out of town for a while. You need to start thinking about protecting yourself.''

Because the police sure as hell can't do it. Isn't that what she was saying? I took a deep breath. ''I'll think about it.''

''Good. Now you take care,'' the detective said in a surprisingly gentle voice. Then she hung up to get back to her crime scene.

I stared at the receiver for what seemed like a long time.

Then I phoned the center to arrange for a leave of absence.

The process was simpler than I'd expected. Since I reported directly to Dr. Cody, the center director, I only needed his permission. I phoned him to see if he'd agree. A plump, avuncular psychiatrist in his early sixties, Dr. Cody told me to take as much time as I needed to "recover from your trauma." This was one of the real advantages of working at the center, I thought, as I hung up: the pay might be substandard, but the empathy level was high.

My next step was getting the necessary paperwork into human resources. Donna Hubbard, predictably, was less understanding than Dr. Cody had been. "You know you can continue to take sick leave until you've recuperated, Liz. Then, when you're in a better frame of mind, the two of us can discuss this option, as well as who will handle your work responsibilities while you're gone."

As politely as possible I told her I didn't think my frame of mind was likely to change, and I'd be in tomorrow to fill out the leave papers. The shot about my work responsibilities had hit home, but I reminded myself that my dying on the job wasn't conducive to optimal productivity either.

By that evening, though, I was starting to have some doubts about my decision. Although my sister had practically leaped up and down with glee when she heard I'd finally decided to go out of town for a while (i.e., taken her advice), I was starting to feel like a bona fide wimp. A few nasty letters and a mugging and old Liz heads for the city limits.

I said as much to Nick when he arrived with a mushrooms-and-black-olives pizza. "Sweetheart, think of it this way," he said in the tone of voice of a man who has won a battle but does not want to rub it in. "You may only be on leave for a couple of weeks, the same amount of time you'd be on vacation. Maybe next week the police will be able to press charges against John Hill and he'll be back in jail."

"So you think he did it?"

"I think you're in danger from him, and I'll feel a whole lot better when he's back in jail."

"But do you think he killed Gina and Nat?"

"I don't know. I wish to hell I did."

I chewed on my pizza, thinking about living in his aunt's rustic cabin in the hill country. Nick and I had spent many weekends there in the past year. It was a lovely, tranquil setting, one in which I'd have time to think things through, and to write. "But what happens if the police *don't* find the killer, and John Hill never goes to jail?" I could be at the cabin for months, going completely bonkers amidst the pastoral serenity.

Nick smiled, leaned over to pat my hand. "Then you can finish your entire novel."

I went to the mental health center the next afternoon, driving back with Amanda after we had lunch. Nick insisted on picking me up for the ride home. In the intervening four hours I could fill out the paperwork for my leave and tie up as many loose ends as possible.

It seemed strange to be back in the center, even though I'd been gone less than a week. To get to my office I had to walk past the stairwell where John Hill had leaped out at me. I could feel my heart thudding, my palms starting to sweat as I approached the stairs. Taking a deep breath, I looked straight ahead and hurried to my office.

The first thing I did when I got inside was grab my correspondence file. What if I'd tossed Jean's letter instead of keeping it? But no, there it was: the snotty little note accusing me of distorting what she'd told me. Rereading it brought back the skinny, sharp-featured woman with the hysterical edge to her voice. I imagined her tiptoeing around John Hill, trying to gauge his mood, praying she wouldn't provoke him.

I studied Jean's small, tight, left-slanting handwriting and felt a sharp stab of disappointment. There was no way she'd written the letter to Gina. That J. H.'s handwriting was large, rounded, and slanted to the right.

I told myself it didn't matter, that probably the letter had nothing to do with Gina's death. Who knows, Gina might have received J. H.'s letter years ago. And even if I had been able to show it was Jean Hill who'd written Gina, Maria Ramirez had already said the letter couldn't prove that John had killed Gina. Nevertheless, I couldn't help feeling I'd driven down still another dead-end street.

I spent the next couple of hours returning phone calls, filling out leave forms, and talking to coworkers who stopped in my office to inquire about my health and assure me that no, really I didn't look bad at all.

I was on the phone when I heard laughter in the hallway. I glanced up and saw two teenage girls I didn't recognize, one tall and gangly, with curly auburn hair, the other shorter and heavier with oily brown hair that hung limply to her shoulders. And suddenly I knew whose handwriting I'd recognized in the letter to Gina.

"Got to go. Talk to you soon," I told the printer I'd been talking to. Then, with mounting excitement, I dialed Missy Gould's extension.

"I know this sounds kind of off-the-wall, Missy," I began, "but do you have a couple of minutes to talk to me?"

I knew how hectic things could get at the adult clinic and crossed my fingers that no patients were now standing at the reception desk waiting for Missy's assistance.

"Sure," Missy said. "What do you need?"

Probably this was just another long shot, I cautioned myself as I told Missy what was on my mind. Still I needed to ask these questions, even if I couldn't figure out yet what the answers meant.

"Yes, I know you weren't good friends, but I figured Lauren might have mentioned something," I said, wondering if I'd ventured onto another dead end. "She did? Was that recently, say, in the last six months?"

I listened and jotted notes on what she told me. "What do you mean she sounded real out of it on the phone?" I stopped writing. "Lauren said she was stoned?" Well, Lauren should know stoned when she heard it.

I figured I'd extracted all the information Missy knew. Any second now she was going to say, "And why did you want to know this, Liz?"

"Missy, I'm sorry. Someone just walked in for an interview. Got to go. Thanks again for the help." I hung up.

When I turned around Donna Hubbard was standing in the doorway. Had she been listening to the conversation? I couldn't tell by her face. It was as inscrutable as ever.

"I wanted to see if you had the leave forms ready yet," she said, walking in.

"I left them on your desk about half an hour ago."

"Oh, I was in a meeting and haven't been back to the office." To my surprise, Donna sat down on the chair next to my desk. "So how are you feeling?" she asked with a smile. "We've all been worried about you."

"I'm feeling better, thanks." I moved my arm to cover

my page of notes. ''Still achy and tired, but a lot better than I was a few days ago.''

I waited for Donna to launch into her don't-shirk-your-work-responsibilities spiel, but she didn't. Instead she invited me to dinner.

''Jennifer came home for the weekend, and she was telling me how much she'd like to see you,'' Donna said. ''Last night she was talking about the great conversations the two of you used to have over lunch. I realize this is terribly short notice, but Jenny is going back to Austin tomorrow night, and she has her heart set on seeing you.''

I smiled. ''I always enjoyed talking to Jennifer; she's a great kid. But I really can't tonight. Nick is coming to pick me up at 5:15, and I'm feeling so exhausted I wouldn't be good company anyway. Maybe the next time Jennifer comes to town we can get together.''

''Oh, Jenny will be *so* disappointed. Are you sure you can't come just for a little while? You can have a couple pieces of pizza and then go home to bed. Jenny or I will be happy to drive you home.''

The conversation was making me uneasy. ''That's really very kind of you,'' I said in my best, brooking-no-nonsense voice, ''but I think I'll have to pass for tonight.'' What I thought, but didn't say, was that Jennifer hadn't spoken to me or written me a word in eighteen months; I figured she could wait a few months longer to see me. ''Maybe we can talk on the phone before she leaves.''

Donna stood up and pushed my office door closed. She reached for something in the pocket of her navy jacket. ''I don't think so.''

She was pointing a gun directly at my head.

Chapter Twenty-five

"FIRST," DONNA SAID, KEEPING HER REVOLVER LEVeled at me, "we're going to cover the ground rules. We are going to walk to my car now. If you try running or yelling for help, I promise you I'll shoot you. Understand?"

I believed her. Her cold gray eyes seemed quite capable of killing without a moment's deliberation. I nodded, unable to speak.

Donna backed to the door and grabbed the handle with her free hand. She opened the door and peered up and down the hall. "There's no one out there to help you, so you can forget that particular idea."

But that didn't mean someone wouldn't be there momentarily. It was only 4:05. People were always wandering down the hall, going to the cafeteria for a candy bar or a Coke. "What's going on, Donna?" I asked, stalling for time. "Why are you doing this?"

"You'll see soon enough." She grabbed my shoulder and shoved me out the door.

There was still no one in sight. Where the hell was everyone?

"Get moving," Donna hissed in my ear.

We turned right, took the hallway at a slow jog, past the cafeteria, out the back door. No one was in the parking lot either.

Donna was so close behind me I could hear her breathe. Should I try to swivel and knock the gun out of her hand? Execute one of the karate kicks I'd learned last year when I was taking tae kwon do? I'd once read that a victim's chance of long-term survival decreased markedly the minute she got into her abductor's car.

As if she could read my mind, Donna jabbed the gun into my back. "Don't even *think* about trying to get away."

We stopped next to her navy Pontiac, parked at the back of the lot. As Donna unlocked the passenger door, I searched frantically for other people, someone who could hear my screams. "Get in," Donna commanded.

I did. She slammed the door shut.

As she walked in front of the car, I grabbed the handle. Pushed open my door.

"I wouldn't do that," Donna said from the opposite doorway. "At least not if I wanted to stay alive." This time her smile was real—a look of pure malice.

Keeping her gun aimed at me, she slid into the driver's seat. "And now, Liz," she said, "you're going to visit your good friend Jennifer."

We drove out of the medical center in silence. Now I saw people everywhere: medical staff, a family probably visiting a hospitalized relative. Their very presence mocked me. Surrounded by onlookers, I was being kidnapped from one of the most congested areas in Houston.

Twenty minutes earlier I'd been elated that I figured out who J. H. was. Now I wondered if the discovery had come too late.

J. H.: Jennifer Hubbard. Jennifer with the ready laugh, the freckles and curly red hair. It was her handwriting that had looked familiar, handwriting which two summers ago

I'd seen quite often. From what Missy had told me, it sounded as if Jennifer had gotten involved with drugs in college. If that was true, I could see Donna putting her daughter in a drug treatment program in Austin. And hadn't Gina once worked at a drug rehab unit at a private psychiatric hospital? Suppose Gina had counseled Jennifer. Did that mean that Jennifer/J. H. was now dead? And had Donna killed Gina in retaliation?

"Uh, what's this all about, Donna?" I asked in a shaky voice. "Am I really going to see Jennifer?" Was Jennifer alive?

Donna didn't even bother to look at me. "You'll find out soon enough," she said, staring straight ahead.

And what was my part in this scenario? If Donna blamed Gina for her harsh treatment of Jennifer in rehab, what did she blame me for? From what I remembered, I'd never been anything other than kind to Jennifer. I certainly had never encouraged her to use drugs. And what about Nat? Had Donna killed him too? I vaguely remembered Jennifer going out on a few dates with Nat the summer she'd worked at the center, but I never thought the romance was serious. Hardly a reason to murder the man.

Donna drove quickly down Holcombe, weaving in and out of traffic. She turned right on Kirby, cruising by the little shops in the Village, the fast-food restaurants near the freeway. Then she turned right again, onto the feeder lane to the Southwest Freeway.

Where was she going? Donna's home—at least the home where she and Jennifer used to live—was in Meyerland. In the opposite direction we were heading. Donna was driving toward downtown. Was it possible we were meeting Jennifer at some downtown restaurant? If, that is, we were meeting her at all.

Donna did not turn off at any of the downtown freeway exits. Instead she headed straight. Past the downtown skyscrapers, past the huge, modernistic George R. Brown Convention Center. Where the hell was she taking me?

"Where *is* Jennifer?" I asked. We were rapidly heading out of town.

This time Donna turned to look at me. "Shut up." She was not smiling.

I could feel my palms get sweaty, feel my heart hammering. It was time to stop thinking of explanations. Time to start concentrating on escapes.

I should have thrown myself out the door when we were still in the medical center. Donna had been driving fairly slowly then, and it was at least possible that some passerby would have come to my rescue. My bruises and aching ribs had made me not want to risk further injuries, had made me want to believe Donna really was taking me to see Jennifer. A stupid, and possibly fatal, mistake. What chance did I have of surviving a fall out of a car now, when Donna was going seventy? And even if I didn't die from the fall, chances were good I'd be hit by another car.

We were at the outskirts of Houston now, heading toward Conroe. Was it possible that Jennifer was living somewhere out here? Perhaps she'd dropped out of college and found a job in one of the smaller towns outside of Houston. Or perhaps this ride had nothing at all to do with Jennifer. Perhaps Donna was just driving out to the country so she could shoot me and dump my body in some overgrown field.

Did this mean Donna was my hate-mail correspondent?

She certainly had enough opportunity to slip into my office and leave her notes. No one who saw her would think twice about Donna leaving a paper on my desk. Donna, with her arrogant disdain for the rest of humanity, would probably have enjoyed the game. Relished my frustration and fear. Hadn't she always known she was a superior being?

But why me? That was the part that didn't make sense. What had I ever done to Donna? Certainly I was aware there was little love lost between the two of us, but the letters I'd received pointed to some specific crime: You'll pay for what you did. I couldn't recall having done anything to Donna.

So who said this had to be rational? Maybe her dislike was enough of a crime. My not agreeing with her, my questioning her judgment, my not bowing and scraping every time she spoke. Firing objectionable employees was so difficult these days. Sometimes drastic means were called for.

Donna eased over into the right lane of the freeway. She was getting ready to exit.

This was my chance. Staring straight ahead, I inched my hand over to the seat-belt button. Finally I found it and—hoping Donna did not possess superhuman peripheral vision—pushed. With my left hand I held the now-loosened seat belt in place.

The car was on the feeder now. Up ahead was a stoplight. Two cars and a white pickup were waiting for the light to turn. I prayed that at least one of the vehicles contained a Good Samaritan. And that we'd get a red light.

Donna slammed on the brake as our light turned yellow. I let go of the seat belt and grabbed for the door handle.

The door was locked! Donna must have locked it from the driver's side. Frantically I pulled at the door button.

It was too late. Grabbing me by the hair, Donna yanked my head back. Her clenched fist slammed into my broken nose.

I shrieked in agony.

"Don't even try it," she snarled, her face inches from mine. "If you'd gotten out of this car I would have shot you in the back, then driven away. Don't imagine for a minute that I'd have to think twice about killing you."

I believed her. The pain from my nose was excruciating. I told myself I had to ignore it, I needed to think. To transcend the pain.

Right.

Donna started driving again, turning right onto a narrow two-lane road, then slowing down, turning right again. Through the tears in my eyes I saw the outline of a large brick building set far back from the road. A hospital or medical facility of some kind.

"Jennifer is *here*?" I asked. What did I have to lose? She was going to shoot me anyway.

"That's right. I told you we were going to visit her." Donna's tone was matter-of-fact, her MBA voice. But when she turned toward me I could see the hatred in her eyes. "In case you're thinking of trying to get away again, next time I shoot first and talk later. And I'm a very good shot."

I could read the sign on the front of the building now, Coastal Psychiatric Hospital. A private psychiatric hospital that every year sent me their four-color brochure detailing their extensive—and very expensive—therapeutic programs.

Had Jennifer suffered some kind of psychotic breakdown? The young woman I remembered was shy and perhaps a bit immature for her age. But I hadn't sensed any major emotional problems, just normal teenaged angst and a strong (and very understandable) desire to break free from her overbearing mother.

"Is Jennifer, uh, ill?"

"Shut up!" Donna drove into the half-empty lot and parked her car in the far corner. "You ask too many damn questions."

I'd been told that before, though never before at gunpoint. Silently, my hand clutching my nose, I listened as Donna gave me her instructions: We were going into the hospital now, going to visit Jennifer. Donna would be right behind me at all times, carrying her gun in the large pocket of her suit jacket. If I tried anything—tried to run away or call for help—she would shoot me.

Donna grabbed my left arm and marched me to the back entrance of the hospital. I could feel the muzzle of her revolver jab me in the back. "We're walking to the elevator. Straight ahead."

The inside of the hospital managed to be both opulent and cold with marble floors, lots of elaborate flower arrangements, and several huge abstract oil paintings in shades of gray and mauve and pink: soothing colors. Your health-care dollars at work.

Donna ignored the sleepy-eyed receptionist at the desk and pointed us toward the elevator. "Can I help you?" the girl, who looked like this might be her after-school job, called after us.

"No, you may not," Donna snapped. "We're visiting a patient."

As the elevator doors opened Donna pushed me inside. She jabbed a floor number—four—then waited, glowering in silence until the elevator stopped.

We stepped out onto a corridor that was less opulent, more generic-institution-looking. Donna grabbed my arm again and led me to a locked door. She pushed a red button immediately to the right of the door.

Jennifer was in a locked ward? I waited for a nurse to peer through a glass partition, then buzz us inside.

"Hello, Mrs. Hubbard. How you doin' tonight?" The nurse was genial, black, carrying a lot of extra weight on her hips. She looked calm and competent, a woman who could handle a crisis. How could I break away from Donna long enough to summon her help?

"I'm fine, thanks." Donna's voice had lost its harsh edge. "How did Jennifer do today?" For the first time in the ten years I'd known her, Donna sounded vulnerable.

The nurse shook her head. "It wasn't one of her good days, poor little thing." She nodded her head in the direction of a big room at the end of the hall. "She's in the activity room now. Why don't you go see her?"

The big nurse looked inquisitively in my direction, clearly wondering who I was. I tried to maintain eye contact, to somehow signal her, but Donna was shoving me down the hall toward the activity room. "Thanks, Pearl," she called.

I didn't know what I expected. The room was big, carpeted, with couches and chairs upholstered in the same muted grays and mauves as downstairs. At one end of the room was a big-screen TV with several glassy-eyed viewers.

What shocked me was Jennifer. She was sitting in a wheelchair by the window. Her face was thinner than I remembered. Despite some kind of belt holding her in the chair, her body slumped forward. She seemed to be staring at something on the floor.

"Jenny." Her mother rushed forward, kneeling on the floor so she could peer into her daughter's face.

Jennifer did not seem to hear her.

If I'd been smart I would have chosen that moment to turn and run, screaming for the friendly nurse by the locked door. It was the only time in the last hour that Donna had been further than a foot away from me.

I was too horrified to move.

At that moment Donna raised her head and waved me over. "Come see what you did, Liz," she said.

Chapter Twenty-six

"WHAT *I'VE* DONE?" I STOOD IN FRONT OF JENNIFER, gazing down at her in undisguised horror.

Jennifer remained transfixed by something on the pale gray carpet. She seemed oblivious to both of us.

Donna reached for her daughter's hand. "Jennifer, sweetie," she said in a soft, pleading voice. "It's Mommy, Jenny."

Jennifer did not respond. Her hand lay limply in Donna's. Her large green eyes—eyes which once had been so animated when she talked—now seemed unfocused.

"What's wrong with her?" I whispered to Donna. Certainly this condition was not the result of casual drug use. Had Jennifer been in some kind of accident? Or had she been ravaged by a degenerative disease? And how could any of these hideous possibilities be my fault?

At first I thought Donna wasn't going to answer. Eyes dark with pain, she kept staring at Jennifer, patting her hand, as if she thought the sheer force of her personality could will her daughter to respond.

"It was a car accident," Donna said so quietly that I had to lean forward to hear her. She looked up at me, her face harsh. "She drove off a mountain road outside of Austin."

"Oh, God." For a moment I was envisioning it. Jennifer inside the car, hurtling down into space. Then the crash.

I forced my mind to stop there. I couldn't bear to contemplate it now. I focused instead on the other topic: What did I have to do with this accident? During the summer Jennifer worked at the center she and I had talked about Austin sometimes when we had lunch together. Had I suggested that Jennifer drive on that particular road? It was possible. I'd mentioned several places around Austin that she should check out: Zilker Park, Mount Bonnell, McKinney Falls State Park. There were hills near all of them. Was Donna blaming me because her daughter had had a terrible accident on the way to visiting some sight I'd recommended? Maybe she thought that Jennifer would have been home safe in her apartment if she hadn't been checking out some of my old hangouts.

It wasn't rational, but the sight of this limp young body and the dead eyes did not invite rational discourse, only a howl of rage and anguished breast-beating. Why? Why? How could this tragedy have occurred? How could a split second's mistake—a skid through a curve in the road, a foolhardy burst of speed in bad driving conditions—transform a vibrant, intelligent young woman into this obscene shell of her former self?

Donna stood up. She walked over to a tired-looking nurse who was dispensing medication to the patients and asked her something. Donna listened, nodded, then returned to the two of us.

"We're going to take Jennifer for a walk on the grounds," she said to me. "The fresh air will do her good. She doesn't get out much." She squatted down and in a quiet voice repeated the information to her daughter.

And what was Donna's plan for me? Now that I'd seen her daughter, what was left on Donna's agenda? Would she return me to the center parking lot or drive me home, just as if I'd come voluntarily? Perhaps that was all that she wanted: that I see Jennifer.

But did people often kidnap someone at gunpoint, then say, "Okay, you're free to go home now"? Especially when this particular kidnapper had sent me three notes promising retribution. As much as I would have liked to believe otherwise, I doubted that Donna Hubbard viewed coming here as appropriate payment for her daughter's injuries. Assuming, of course, that was what she was accusing me of.

"Come along, Liz." Donna grasped my elbow. "Why don't you push Jennifer's wheelchair." She said it in the level, rather imperious voice she used at the office, giving me no clue what was coming next.

The two of us walked out of the ward. Donna told the nurse who unlocked the door that we wouldn't be gone long.

I wanted to believe her.

We rode down in the elevator in silence. When the door opened I pushed the wheelchair along the marble floor, past the bland, institution-sized paintings, the pastel furniture.

Outside the air seemed cooler; the wind had picked up. "Turn left," Donna commanded.

We headed toward a large expanse of grass, divided into small gardens with wooden benches. A gravel trail connected the gardens. I imagined a color advertisement for the hospital showing a smiling family visiting a patient by the blooming rose garden. The patient, of course, would look as if there was nothing at all wrong with her.

Quickly I searched the grounds, looking for other people. No one was in sight. No families sat outside visiting. No employees were taking their breaks in the gardens.

"I guess you're wondering how this happened to Jennifer," Donna said in the tone of voice of someone discussing the weather.

She didn't seem to require a response. Donna continued as we headed down the gravel trail, "The way I see it, everything started two summers ago when Jennifer worked at the center. I view that summer as the start of a downward spiral for Jennifer. It was as if in a few short months all my years of work with her, all my dreams for her, were destroyed."

I didn't have a clue what she was alluding to. Had the horror of her only child's accident made Donna lose touch with reality? Perhaps she had to invent reasons for this horrible tragedy in order to comprehend it.

"Did you know that Nat Ryan seduced Jennifer that summer?" she asked.

I shook my head. I knew that Jennifer had gone out with Nat a few times, but I never thought Jennifer was especially besotted by him. Not, say, the way Lauren later was. "You mean Nat slept with Jennifer?" I asked. I wasn't sure that Donna's and my definition of seduction were the same.

"I mean," Donna said in an icy voice, "that Nat allowed my daughter to fall in love with him and let her believe that he felt the same way about her. Then, when he was tired of their little affair, he blithely announced that it was over. He broke her heart."

Hadn't Olivia said basically the same thing about the way Nat treated her? "And Jennifer was very upset about this?"

"She was devastated." Donna's eyes flashed in the light from the back of the hospital. "It was then that she started using drugs. Marijuana, at first. I found out only recently that it was Lauren—her *good friend*—who supplied her with drugs. I always wondered where Jennifer was getting them. When I found a bag of pot in her underwear drawer, I immediately confronted her. She cried and told me it would never happen again. She said she was just experimenting, she only wanted to see what all the fuss was about.''

Donna glanced down at the back of her daughter's slumped head. She suddenly looked old and exhausted. ''But it did happen again. As soon as she was away from me in Austin.''

''So Jennifer was using drugs when she had her accident?'' I asked. It would explain a lot.

Donna ignored me. She continued with her story, a speaker refusing to budge from her prepared script. ''I didn't realize it for a while. I thought everything was fine. I talked to Jennifer regularly on the phone and she sounded very involved in her classes, adjusting well, making friends. Then I saw her first grades: a lot of C's, and one D—and this from a former straight-A student. Suddenly I felt suspicious about why Jenny never wanted to come home on weekends. And the few times she did come home I never saw her. She was always off with some friend—frequently Lauren—and she was always begging me for money.''

I was starting to see how all the pieces fit together. My stomach began to churn. I gulped in cold air, trying to calm myself down. I needed to be clearheaded now to figure out what I had to do.

We were far behind the hospital now, heading toward a giant oak tree and the last of the little gardens. I still didn't see a soul within shouting distance.

Donna continued her story, oblivious to my reaction. Telling how eventually she realized the severity of Jennifer's drug problem—no longer just pot, but now cocaine too. Donna had put Jennifer in a highly recommended, in-patient drug treatment program in Austin. It hadn't worked. Within weeks of leaving the program, Jennifer was back on drugs. In one of her last conversations with her mother, Jennifer had told of a bullying drug counselor at the program, a tyrant who wouldn't let up on her, who came down on Jennifer for the slightest infraction of the rules.

"Gina?" I whispered. Donna nodded. Gina, the abrasive therapist who believed you sometimes had to push clients to do the right thing. Gina, the antidrug fanatic.

Who Donna had murdered with a syringe full of heroin: retribution for her daughter's drive off a cliff.

And what about Lauren? Was it a coincidence that she too had died of a drug overdose? Suddenly I had to know. "Did you kill Lauren?"

"Of course." Donna's tone was matter-of-fact. "She supplied my daughter with drugs. She introduced them to her."

"How did you do it?" I needed to keep her talking.

"It was surprisingly easy to buy illegal drugs—the heroin and LSD—from clients at our substance abuse clinic. I put the LSD in Lauren's Diet Coke. I stopped at her apartment after work that night, and the two of us had a soda and a little chat. I knew she was going to her parents' house that night, that she'd be driving on the freeway soon." Donna paused to look at me, her eyes cold, demented. "I like to think she had an experience similar to Jennifer's: driving while under the influence."

And what fitting punishment was she planning for me?

As if she sensed what I was thinking, Donna said, "And what about you? I'm sure a lot of people would say that what you did was innocent enough, just convincing Jennifer to go away to school. What harm was there in that?"

The trail had now dead-ended into the last garden. I parked Jennifer's wheelchair next to one of the wooden benches. The end of the trail: the phrase ran inanely through my head.

Donna pulled the revolver from her jacket pocket. "I had that girl's future planned, Liz. Live at home, go to Houston Baptist University, major in business like I did."

And who cared if that wasn't what Jennifer wanted? I knew how Donna would answer: If she'd done what I told her, Jennifer might be bored, but she'd be fully functioning today.

"But no," Donna continued, her voice harsh. "*You* had to convince my daughter to abandon our plans, major in journalism, not business, go away to school, have some fun on her own." She nodded her head at Jennifer, who was staring blankly at the ground. "She sure had a lot of *fun*, didn't she?"

A noise from the hospital made Donna turn. It was my chance, very probably my last chance.

I shoved Donna to the ground, then took off running. Toward the giant oak and, behind that, the parking lot. Toward the figures in the white uniforms who'd just come outside for a smoke.

I'd made it to the oak when the first shot slammed into the tree trunk, inches from my head. I dove to the ground, yelling for help.

I heard the second shot. Another miss. Then came the scream. Inhuman almost, the kind of keening I'd only heard on the TV news when wives or mothers mourned their casualties of war.

Rolling onto my hands and knees, I turned back to the little garden. Donna Hubbard sat on the ground, holding her daughter's limp, bleeding body. Rocking back and forth, howling her grief.

I saw the two men in white uniforms start running toward Donna and Jennifer. Donna glanced up and saw them too.

"No!" The scream came from my mouth as I saw Donna stick the muzzle of the gun in her own mouth. She was looking at her daughter when she pulled the trigger.

Chapter Twenty-seven

THEY HAD A DOUBLE FUNERAL. DONNA HUBBARD AND the daughter she wanted to mold in her own image, protect from harm, and, failing that, avenge the wrongs done to her.

I almost didn't go. I'd been to too many funerals lately, and I was in no condition to go anywhere. The combination of my physical injuries from John Hill's attack and the emotional residue from Donna's abduction had somehow merged into an achy, paralyzing exhaustion. After giving my statement to the police, I'd gone home and slept for twelve hours. And still felt tired.

But in the end I pulled myself out of bed, got dressed in my navy suit, and came to pay my respects to Jennifer, the shy, smiling summer intern who'd confided in me her secret desire to be a journalist. Also I guess I hoped that coming to the funeral might help me make sense of everything that had happened.

It didn't. The Baptist minister delivered a sermon about God's promise of comfort to the hurt and the grieving. He didn't dwell much on the two women who were going to be buried. Maybe he hadn't known them well. Or maybe he did and was as stunned as the rest of us by what had taken place.

I sat in the pew, feeling numb, surrounded by colleagues

from the mental health center. The women who'd worked with Donna, the clerks and secretaries from human resources, looked the most shell-shocked. Their supervisor, the woman they saw every day, had been a killer?

That shocked disbelief was the response Nick had encountered over and over when he'd interviewed mental health center employees for his story about Donna. I'd read the article in the *Chronicle* yesterday. Essentially it was a factual and fairly restrained account of the murders and Donna's attempt on my life. I refused to be interviewed for it.

My strongest response to the story, though, was my agreement with my colleagues' assessment: Sure, Donna was a tyrant, a rigid, no-nonsense workaholic, but she didn't seem like a murderer. Only minutes before she entered my office last Friday had I even begun to suspect Donna's part in the deaths of my friends.

Amanda O'Neil touched my knee. "Come on. Let's get out of here."

The service, I saw, was over. I hadn't even noticed the mourners—mostly people from the center, interspersed with some teenage friends of Jennifer—filing out of the church.

I wasn't noticing a lot lately. I followed Amanda out of the church.

"Detective Ramirez phoned me this morning," I told Amanda as she backed her Honda out of its parking space. "She wanted me to know that Jean Hill's body has been found, and John is being charged with her murder. He apparently strangled her and then buried her body behind a shack he owns in the country."

Ironically Todd Murdock had helped pin the murder on

Hill. He'd hired a private detective to uncover evidence that Hill had killed Gina. The investigator followed John to an isolated, run-down cabin on the outskirts of Huntsville. Checking out the place after Hill left, he discovered a grassless mound behind the cabin. Not seeing Hill as a likely gardener, the investigator notified the police that he suspected he'd found an unmarked grave.

"So Jean never did run away," Amanda said.

"I always thought she wouldn't voluntarily leave the girls alone with him. No matter how scared she was, Jean would have taken them along with her." Another mother, I thought, who'd tried, but hadn't succeeded, in protecting her children from harm.

"I hope their aunt can keep Jean's girls," I said. "Maybe even adopt them."

"I hope so too. I think I'd like to go visit Rosie and Emily again. Want to come with me this weekend?"

"I think I'll pass this time, but give the girls my love."

"I will." We drove in silence for a few minutes, Amanda snaking through the downtown traffic.

I usually enjoyed seeing downtown Houston: the stark, diagonal lines of the Pennzoil Place skyscraper, the castle-like Alley Theatre, the cylindrical stainless steel fountain of Tranquility Park, Houston's tribute to space flight. It was contemporary and architecturally creative: the embodiment, as the mayor liked to say, of Houston's can-do spirit. But today the only sights I seemed able to focus on were my mental images of Donna's and Jennifer's coffins being lowered into the ground.

"What a horrible, horrible waste!" I said. "Think of it, Amanda. Five people are dead, four of them under thirty-five years old. All as a result of Jennifer having a summer job at the center. If Jennifer had worked somewhere else those couple of months, Nat and Lauren would never even have met her. And if Lauren hadn't offered her drugs, or I hadn't suggested she go away to school in Austin, Gina would probably never have treated her in drug rehab. And maybe Jennifer and Donna would still be living together today while Jennifer went to college in Houston."

"Except eventually Jennifer was going to have problems," Amanda said. "She was going to meet someone else who'd offer her drugs; she'd date somebody else who would break her heart. The problem was she was a fragile girl with a domineering, control freak for a mother. Somewhere down the line Jennifer was going to rebel. Though, you're right, there certainly were tragic consequences to her rebellion."

I gnawed at the inside of my mouth, a barbaric habit I thought I'd broken. "I don't understand how Donna could blame everyone except Jennifer and herself for what happened. Everything was someone else's fault. Jennifer was just this innocent victim."

Amanda sighed. "At some level Donna had to blame herself, and Jennifer too. But the flurry of activity—the poison-pen letters, the murders—probably helped her push away the despair for a while. The planning and executing of her crimes took a great deal of time and attention. It fueled her rage. But once she finished her retribution"—Amanda glanced sideways at me, suddenly realizing she was talking about my life—"she would have had to face her grief, the overwhelming sadness. There was a very good chance she would have lapsed into a major depression."

"So only my still being alive kept her from facing her demons." Maybe that was why Donna had delayed meting out my punishment—not some conviction that I was less guilty than the others, but a suspicion that once I was out of the way, she'd have no more games to win, no more adversaries to demolish.

I had gone over and over the events of the day Donna abducted me, trying to piece together what had happened behind my back once I started running away from her. Donna had shot at me and missed. Had she then spotted the hospital workers and realized that she couldn't get away with my murder, that this time she was going to be caught? Probably Donna had reasoned that if she were in prison no one would be there to visit Jennifer or to pay for her expensive hospital care. Death, she'd decided, would be preferable for both of them. That seemed the most likely explanation. But who could tell if it was the correct one? Perhaps all along Donna had intended to end both of their lives after she'd killed all those she held responsible for Jennifer's accident. And now I was the only one of those people still living.

We drove the rest of the way in a melancholy silence, interrupted only when Amanda pulled into my apartment's parking lot. "You're sure you don't want me to come up for a while?" she asked, peering into my face with those intense, hazel eyes.

"No, Mother, I'm fine." I attempted a smile. "Really, Amanda, I just want to go take a nap." On many levels, the funeral had left me exhausted.

Amanda nodded. "That sounds like a good idea." She leaned over to give me a hug. "Call me if you need anything, even if it's just to talk."

I assured her I would, though right now talking was

about the last thing I wanted to do. Lately the only activity that held any appeal was sleeping.

That was just what I was doing when Nick came by. The sound of a key turning in the front door lock awakened me. "What time is it?" I asked, sitting up in bed as he entered the bedroom.

Nick checked his watch. "It's 5:20. I left work early."

He sat on the edge of my bed and draped an arm around me. "I have a surprise for you." From behind his back he produced an oversized envelope and handed it to me.

I opened the envelope. Inside were glossy travel brochures, all apparently to various tropical locations.

"Look them over and pick the one you like best." He correctly interpreted my wary look. "No, it's not a honeymoon. Just a vacation. I think we both could use one."

I glanced through the brochures, which all pictured couples sprawled on sandy beaches or frolicking in intensely turquoise bodies of water.

"Just imagine lying on the beach, your body baking in the sun while you listen to the waves lap against the shore," Nick said.

"Reading trashy novels while sipping rum drinks with little umbrellas in them," I said, getting into it.

"At night sitting in some open-air restaurant, surrounded by palm trees, listening to a reggae band," Nick continued.

But then I thought of all the papers piling up on my desk, the phone calls to answer, the meetings I needed to attend. I started to say I'd already missed more than a week of work and needed to get back to the center. Started to say I was too sore, too tired, too depressed to go on a vacation.

I needed to act responsibly. People were counting on me. I couldn't let them down—could I?

I gazed into the intensely blue eyes of the man I might or might not marry. I handed him a brochure. "Jamaica," I said.